W9-AYA-677

USA TODAY Bestselling Author

DELORES FOSSEN

MASON

HARLEQUIN®
entertain, enrich, inspire™

Recycling programs
for this product may
not exist in your area.

ISBN-13: 978-0-373-69638-3

MASON

www.Harlequin.com

Printed in U.S.A.

ABOUT THE AUTHOR

Imagine a family tree that includes Texas cowboys, Choctaw and Cherokee Indians, a Louisiana pirate and a Scottish rebel who battled side by side with William Wallace. With ancestors like that, it's easy to understand why *USA TODAY* bestselling author and former air force captain Delores Fossen feels as if she were genetically predisposed to writing romances. Along the way to fulfilling her DNA destiny, Delores married an air force top gun who just happens to be of Viking descent. With all those romantic bases covered, she doesn't have to look too far for inspiration.

Books by Delores Fossen

CAST OF CHARACTERS

Deputy Mason Ryland—Dark and brooding, most people fear him, but he's hiding wounds so deep he believes they'll never heal—until he crosses paths with his new horse trainer, Abbie. Mason is thrown into a whirlwind of danger with the highest stakes, including falling hard for a woman he can't have.

Abbie Baker—She has deadly secrets, and one of them puts her on a collision course not just with her boss, Mason, but with the entire Ryland clan and a killer who just won't stop.

Boone Ryland—He abandoned his family two decades ago, and his sons despise him for it. But does Boone know the truth that can save them, or is he the reason someone is gunning for all the Rylands?

Vernon Ferguson—He's had a vendetta against Abbie for most of her life, and he's not saying much about his untimely arrival in Silver Creek.

Rodney Stone—A lawyer and longtime friend of the late Senator Ford Herrington, who always swore he'd get back at the Rylands for an old wrong.

Ace Chapman—He has a reputation as a hired gun, but he also might know who's behind the attempts to kill Abbie and the Rylands.

Nicole Manning—She was Senator Herrington's lover, and she claims she has no plans to carry out her former lover's wishes from beyond the grave.

Chapter One

The scream woke Deputy Mason Ryland.

His eyes flew open, and Mason stumbled from the sofa in his office where he'd fallen asleep. He reached for his shirt but couldn't find it. He had better luck with the Smith & Wesson handgun that he'd left on his desk.

He threw open his office door and caught the scent of something he darn sure didn't want to smell on the grounds of his family's ranch.

Smoke.

The wispy gray streaks coiled around him, quickly followed by a second scream and a loud cry for help.

Mason went in the direction of both the smoke and the voice, racing out into the chilly October night air. He wasn't the only one who'd been alerted. A handful of his ranch hands were running toward the cabin-style guesthouse about a hundred yards away. It was on fire, the orangey flames licking their way up the sides and roof. And the place wasn't empty.

His newly hired horse trainer, Abbie Baker, was staying there.

That got Mason running even harder. So did another shout for help. Oh, yeah, that shout was coming from the guesthouse all right.

"Call the fire department," he yelled to one of the ranch hands.

Mason also shouted out for someone to call his brothers as well even though they would soon know anyway. All five of them, their wives and their children lived in the family home or on the grounds of the ranch.

Mason made it to the guesthouse ahead of the others, and he tried to pick through the smoke and the embers flicking through the night air. He hurried to the sound of his trainer's pleas for help.

And he cursed when he saw her.

Abbie was in the doorway, her body half in and half out of the house, and what was left of the door was on her back, anchoring her in place.

The smoke was thick and black, and the area was already hot from the flames, but Mason fought his way through just as one of the ranch hands caught up with him. Rusty Burke. Together, they latched on to the door and started to drag it off Abbie. Not easily. It was heavy and bulky, and it didn't help that the flames were snapping at them.

Mason didn't usually think in terms of worst-case scenarios, but he had a split-second thought that his new trainer might burn to death. The possibility gave him a much-needed jolt of adrenaline, and Rusty and he threw the door off her. In the same motion, Mason latched on to her arm and dragged her away from the guesthouse.

"I couldn't get out," she said, her voice clogged with smoke and fear.

"You're out now," he let her know.

Out but not necessarily safe. The ranch hands were already there with the hoses, but he doubted the house would stand much longer. If it collapsed, Abbie could still be burned or hurt from the flying debris.

"Are the horses okay?" she asked. Mason was more than a little surprised that she'd think of the animals at a time like this.

"They're fine." At least he was pretty sure of that. "This is the only building on fire."

Mason scooped her up, and she looked at him. It was pitch-dark, probably two or three in the morning, but thanks to the flames and the hunter's moon, he saw her eyes widen. A single word left her mouth.

"No."

Mason didn't have time to question that *no* before she started struggling. She wasn't a large woman, five-five at the most and on the lean side, but she managed to pack a punch when she rammed her elbow against his bare chest. He cursed and put her in a death grip so she couldn't fight her way out of his arms.

"I'm trying to save you," he reminded her, and he added more profanity when she didn't stop fighting.

Abbie was probably still caught up in the fear and the adrenaline, but Mason was finding it a little hard to be sympathetic with the cold rocky ground biting into his bare feet and with her arms and legs waggling around.

"We have to get away from the fire," he snarled.

Those wide frightened eyes looked at the flames, and she stopped struggling just long enough for Mason to get a better grip on her.

He started running toward the ranch office where lately he'd been spending most of his days and nights because of the heavy workload. He could deposit Abbie there and hurry back to see if the guesthouse could be saved. He wasn't hopeful, especially because the ranch wasn't exactly in city limits. It would take the fire department a good twenty minutes to reach them.

The door to his office and quarters was still open, and

he hurried inside, flipped on the lights with his elbow and placed her on the sofa. Mason looked down at her, to make sure she wasn't injured.

She didn't appear to be.

Visibly shaken, yes. Trembling, too. Pale and breathing way too fast. All normal responses under the circumstances.

Her eyes met his again, and Mason saw the fear that was still there. And maybe something else that he couldn't quite put his finger on.

"Did you try to kill me?" she asked.

That single question seemed to be all she could muster because she groaned, closed her eyes, and the back of her head dropped against the sofa.

Mason huffed. That definitely wasn't something he expected to hear her say. He'd been a deputy for fifteen years, and his employee no doubt knew it. Even though most people were leery of him because…well, because he wasn't a friendly sort, they didn't usually accuse him of arson or attempted murder.

"Why would I set this fire?" he demanded.

Abbie opened her mouth, closed it and shook her head. She also dodged his gaze. "I'm not sure what I'm saying right now. I thought I was going to die."

Mason guessed that was a normal response, but he was beginning to get a bad feeling about this. "How did the fire start?"

Abbie shook her head again. "I'm not sure. I woke up, and there was smoke all around me. I tried to get to the door, but I started coughing and couldn't see." She paused, shivered. "When I got to the door and opened it, it fell on me." Another pause. "Or something."

"Or something?" he pushed.

Oh, man. The bad feeling was getting worse, and Mason

blamed it on that stupid question. Was there a nonstupid reason that she thought someone had tried to kill her, or was this the ramblings of a woman whose mind had been clouded with fear and adrenaline?

"Or something," she repeated.

Abbie pushed her light brown hair from her face. Long hair, he noticed. Something he hadn't realized because she always wore it tucked beneath a baseball cap. In fact, he'd thought of her as tomboyish, but there wasn't anything boyish or tom about the person lying on his sofa. In that paper-thin pale blue gown, she looked like a woman.

An attractive one.

Something Mason wished like the devil he hadn't noticed. She worked for him, and he didn't tread down that path. Business and sex never sat well with him.

"Did you leave the stove on?" he pressed.

But all he got was another head shake—something else that didn't please him. He wanted some answers here, and he wanted something to tamp down that bad feeling in his gut. However, the knock on his already-open door had him shifting in that direction.

It was his ranch hand Rusty. The lanky young man was out of breath and looked on the verge of blurting something out before his attention landed on Abbie. He motioned for Mason to meet him outside.

Mason looked at Abbie. "I'll be right back." Yeah, it sounded like a warning and it was. By God, he was going to get those answers and settle this uneasy feeling. He would find out why she'd thought he had tried to kill her.

He stepped outside with Rusty, and when he got a better look at Rusty's face, he pulled the door shut. "More bad news?" But it wasn't exactly a question. Mason could already tell there was.

Rusty nodded. "The guesthouse collapsed. Nothing left to save."

Well, heck. That didn't please Mason, but it could have been much worse. His trainer could have gotten killed.

Abbie could have gotten killed, he mentally corrected.

And he cursed himself for thinking of her that way. Mason blamed it on that blasted thin gown and those frightened vulnerable brown eyes.

"There's more," Rusty went on, grabbing Mason's attention.

Mason took a deep breath, ready to hear the news he probably didn't want to hear, but before Rusty could spill it, he saw his brother Grayson hurrying toward them.

Like Mason, his brother was half-dressed. Jeans that he'd probably just pulled on and no shirt. Even half-dressed, Grayson still managed to look as if he were in charge.

And he was.

As the eldest of his five brothers and the Silver Creek town sheriff, Grayson had a way of being in charge just by being there.

"How's the trainer?" Grayson immediately asked.

"Alive," Mason provided. He didn't add the customary *and well* part to that because he wasn't sure that was true. He should probably look to see if she'd had a blow to the head. After all, the door could have hit her when it became unhinged. She might even have a broken bone or two.

"The EMTs are on the way," Grayson explained. He looked at Mason. "Rusty told you about the guesthouse?"

Mason nodded. "It's gone."

Grayson stopped next to him, his breath gusting. Probably because he'd run all the way from the main ranch house. "Yeah. And there was a gas can by the back porch. Rusty managed to pull it out of there before the flames took over."

What the devil? Mason mentally went through the reasons why Abbie would have had a gas can on the porch, and he couldn't immediately think of one. She trained his cutting horses and didn't have anything to do with any ranch equipment that required gasoline.

"Looks like someone could have set the fire," Grayson concluded.

Arson. On the ranch.

The anger slammed through Mason. Even though he had five brothers who were equal owners of the land, the ranch was *his* domain. He ran it. It was what he loved, more than a badge, more than just about anything. And if someone had intentionally burned down the guesthouse with Abbie inside, then that someone was going to pay and pay *hard*.

"It could have been worse," Rusty went on, turning to Grayson. "Mason barely got Abbie out of there in time."

That was true. And Mason went back to Abbie's stupid question.

Did you try to kill me?

Had she seen something or someone? Maybe. And Mason changed that *maybe* to a *probably* after remembering the way she'd looked at him. He was accustomed to people shying out of his way. Used to the uneasiness that he caused with his steely exterior, but Abbie's fear had twisted something inside of him that he hadn't felt before.

The sound of sirens sliced through his anger and thoughts, and all three of them looked in the direction of the road where there were swirls of red-and-blue lights approaching. The fire department, an ambulance and a sheriff's cruiser. Could be one of his brothers, Dade or Gage, in the cruiser, because they were both deputies.

"I'll talk to them," Grayson volunteered. "You stay with the trainer until the EMTs have checked her out."

He would, but while he was doing that, Mason could ask some questions that might help them get to the bottom of all of this.

Grayson and Rusty headed out in the direction of the approaching emergency responders, and Mason threw open his office door. His attention zoomed right to the sofa where he'd left Abbie.

She wasn't there.

Mason looked at the adjoining bathroom. Door closed. And that's probably where she was—maybe crying or falling apart from the inevitable adrenaline crash.

He took a moment to pull on his boots, but when he still couldn't find his shirt, he crossed the large working space and knocked on the bathroom door.

No answer.

So he knocked again, harder this time. "You okay in there?"

Still no answer.

He rethought that crying or falling-apart theory and moved on to one that caused his concern to spike through the roof. Maybe she was unconscious from an injury he hadn't noticed.

No knock this time. Mason kicked down the door and was thankful when it didn't hit her. He looked at the sink first. Not there. Then, the separate toilet area. Not there either. And she darn sure wasn't in the shower.

That's when he noticed the bathroom window was wide-open.

What the devil was going on?

He hurried to the window and looked out. Thanks to that hunter's moon, he saw her. Barely. She was at least thirty yards away, her pale blue gown fluttering in the wind.

Abbie was running as if her life depended on it.

Chapter Two

Abbie didn't take the time to tell herself that it'd been a really bad idea to come to the Ryland ranch. But that's what she would do later. For now, she just had to get out of there as fast as she could and hope that she could somehow make it to safety.

Safety with no car, no money, no shoes.

Clearly, she had some big strikes against her.

Abbie glanced over her shoulder and saw one of the biggest strikes of all. Mason Ryland. Her boss and perhaps the person who wanted her dead.

She'd been a fool to come here, and that foolishness might soon get her killed.

With Mason's footsteps bearing down on her, Abbie didn't give up. She ran, praying that she would make it to the fence before he could grab her. The fence wasn't a sure thing. First, she'd have to scale it and then try to disappear into the thick woods that surrounded the sprawling ranch. But just reaching the fence was her next obstacle.

"Stop!" Mason yelled.

His angry voice tore through the darkness, through her, and she had a terrifying thought.

What if he shot her?

After all, he had a gun. Abbie had seen it when Rusty and he had pulled the door off her. The sight of that weapon and his fierce take-no-prisoners expression had caused her heart to skip a beat or two.

She kept running, her lungs already starved for air, but she wasn't fast enough. With the fence still yards away, Mason grabbed her shoulder and dragged her to a stop before he whirled her around to face him.

"What the hell do you think you're doing?" Mason demanded.

Abbie wanted to demand the same thing, but she couldn't gather enough breath to speak. Mercy, her teeth were chattering from the chilly night air and the fear.

"Well?" he pushed. He looked down at her. At her face. At her gown. At the garment she was wearing over her gown. "And why did you steal my shirt?"

"I borrowed it," Abbie managed to say. She would have done the same to a pair of shoes if she could have found them. She hadn't. So she'd run out of his office barefoot.

He mumbled some more profanity and stared at her as if she'd lost her mind. Maybe she had. But thankfully he didn't shoot her or threaten to do it. That reprieve meant she had a chance to try to talk him out of whatever he was planning to do to her.

"Look, I'll just go," she managed to say after sucking in some more air.

"To heck you will." He kept a punishing grip on her arm. "First, you'll tell me about that fire and why you ran. After that, I can decide if I'll arrest you for arson."

That put some air back in her lungs. "What? Arrest me? I didn't do anything wrong."

Mason gave her another you've-lost-your-mind glare, and those ice-gray eyes drilled into her. Abbie couldn't see the color of his eyes in the darkness, but she knew them well enough from her job interview. Not that he'd given her more than a passing glance in the three days she'd worked for him.

Well, he was doing more than glancing now.

In addition to the glare he'd aimed at her, his gaze kept dropping to her cotton nightgown. It wasn't a garment meant to be provocative, but she felt exposed with Mason's attention on her.

Mason had a way of doing that, she'd learned.

Tall, dark and dangerous with his black hair and hard face. His brothers had those same Ryland looks, but they were softened on their faces and bodies. Not Mason. He looked like an ornery vampire.

Without a shirt.

Added to that were those gunmetal-gray cop's eyes that saw, and had seen, way too much.

Abbie slid her left hand over her chest. Over the silver chain that veed down into her gown and in between her breasts. She couldn't let Mason see the pendant at the end of the chain. If he did, the anger and questions would come at her full blast.

"We can stand out here and freeze our butts off," he continued, "or you can tell me what happened."

Because she couldn't tear out of his grip and because he had that gun, Abbie knew she had to give him some kind of answer. The truth?

Probably not.

Not until she was sure she could trust him, and so far Mason hadn't done anything to make her believe she could. Well, except pull her out of the burning house, but she wasn't sure yet why he'd done that. Maybe her shouts for help had drawn so much attention that he felt he had no choice but to make a show of rescuing her. He probably wouldn't have wanted anyone saying he'd let his trainer burn to death. Even if maybe that's what he'd wanted to happen.

"I already told you I'm not an arsonist," she explained. "I woke up, and the place was already on fire. I tried to get out, but when I made it to the front door, someone pushed me to the ground and shoved the door on me."

"What *someone?*" he challenged.

Abbie shook her head. "I didn't see his face."

He studied her, his glare getting even harder. "So why accuse me then?"

Now, here's where she had to lie. "I was scared. Talking out of my head. I've never come that close to dying."

And that, too, was a lie. A whopper, actually.

Oh, she'd come close all right.

The seconds crawled by, and even though her teeth were still chattering and the goose bumps were crawling all up and down her, that didn't seem to give Mason any urgency. Even though he was no doubt cold, too.

That no-shirt part caught her attention again.

She didn't want to look at him. Okay, she did. Once more she was intrigued by how the Ryland genes could have created this puzzling mix of danger and hotness. Under different circumstances, she might have been attracted to Mason Ryland.

Abbie mentally groaned at that thought. Not good. Thoughts like that could only make this situation worse. And she was already at *worse*. The trick now would be to stop the damage from escalating into a full-blown nightmare.

"I have to get out of here," she blurted out. "I can't stay."

Still no urgency from Mason, and when she tried to move, he snapped her back in place. "You honestly believe someone tried to kill you tonight?"

Abbie thought about her answer. "Yes," she said, even

though she dreaded what he would ask next. She didn't have to wait long.

"Why would someone want to kill you?"

Mason's question hung in the air and was just as smothering and as potentially lethal as the fire and smoke had been. Abbie tried to shrug. "Since I've been here at the ranch, I've had the feeling someone's watching me."

Also the truth.

Without warning, Mason released the grip on her, but he continued that ruthless stare. "Did you tell anyone about this?"

Abbie settled for a head shake.

"Well, you should have," he growled. "We have surveillance cameras all over the ranch, but they're not monitored unless I'm aware there's a problem. I wasn't aware. Plus, there's the part about me being a deputy sheriff. I would have been very interested in knowing that you thought someone might be watching you."

"I'm sorry," Abbie mumbled. But there's no way she could have told him about her suspicions without making Mason and his brothers suspicious. "I'll pack my things…" Except her things had all burned. She was literally wearing everything she owned. "I have to leave," she repeated.

"Not a chance. If the fire was arson, there'll be an investigation. Grayson will need to interview you. There will be paperwork. And I hate paperwork," he added in a gruff mumble.

Grayson, the sheriff. Another set of cop's eyes. Just what she didn't need right now. But she couldn't very well break into a run and expect to get away.

No.

Her best bet was to pretend to cooperate so she could get out of there as fast as possible. Then she could regroup and figure out what to do.

Abbie glanced down at her gown to make sure the pendant was still hidden. It was. "Could I maybe borrow some clothes?"

Mason didn't jump right on that with a resounding yes, but he finally grumbled one under his breath. What he didn't do was stop the staring, and he sure as heck didn't move.

"For the record, I think you're lying about something," he informed her. "Don't know what yet, but I *will* find out. And if you set that fire, so help me—"

"I didn't set it," Abbie snarled back.

"You're willing to have your hands and clothes analyzed for traces of gasoline or some other accelerant?" he snapped.

The question stopped her cold. Under normal circumstances, no, she wouldn't mind. She would even volunteer. But these were far from normal circumstances. She obviously needed to get out of there.

Still, Abbie nodded. "Of course."

Mason stared at her. And stared. Before he finally hitched his shoulder in the direction of the fire and the other ranch buildings. "Come on."

Not exactly a warm and fuzzy invitation, but Abbie was thankful they were walking. Not easily and not very quickly. After all, she was barefoot, and Mason seemed to be as uncomfortable as she was.

"Tell me why you came here," Mason tossed out. A demand that almost caused her heart to stop. Until he added, "Why did you want to work at the Ryland ranch?"

"You asked that in the interview," she reminded him, but Abbie paraphrased the lie to refresh his memory. "You have one of the best track records in the state for cutting horses. I wanted to be part of that."

Mercy, it sounded rehearsed.

He made a gruff sound to indicate he was giving that some thought. Thought smothered with suspicion. "You knew a lot about the ranch before you applied for the job?"

Abbie nodded—cautiously. The man had a way of completely unnerving her. "Sure. I did a lot of reading about it on the internet."

"Like what?" he fired back.

She swallowed hard and hoped her voice didn't crack. "Well, I read the ranch has a solid reputation. Your father, Boone Ryland, started it forty years ago when he was in his early twenties."

Mason stopped and whirled around so quickly that it startled her. He aimed his index finger at her as if he were about to use it to blast her into another county. Then, he turned and started walking again.

"My *father*," he spat out like profanity, "bought the place. That's it. He didn't even have it paid off before he hightailed it out of here, leaving his wife and six sons. A wife who committed suicide because he broke her spirit and cut her to the core. He was a sorry SOB and doesn't deserve to have his name associated with *my* ranch that I've worked hard to build."

The venom stung, even though Abbie had known it was there. She just hadn't known it would hurt this much to hear it said aloud and aimed at her.

"You don't look as much like your father as your brothers do," she mumbled. And before the last word had left her mouth, Abbie knew it had been a Texas-sized mistake.

Mason stopped again, so quickly that she ran right into him. It was like hitting a brick wall. An angry one.

"How the hell would you know that?" Mason demanded.

Oh, mercy.

Think, Abbie, think.

"I saw your father's picture," she settled for saying.

The staring started again. Followed by his glare that even the darkness couldn't conceal. "What picture?" he asked, enunciating each word.

Abbie shook her head and started walking. Or rather, she tried to do that. But Mason caught onto her arm and slung her around to face him.

"What picture?" he repeated.

She searched for a lie he'd believe, one that could get her out of this nightmare that she'd created. But before she could say anything, Mason's gaze snapped to the side.

And he lifted his gun in that direction.

For one horrifying moment, Abbie thought he was going to turn that gun on her, but his attention was focused on a cluster of trees in the distance. The trees were near the fence that Abbie had fought so hard to reach.

Mason stepped in front of her so quickly, she hadn't sensed it coming. He put himself between her and those trees.

"What's wrong?" she asked.

"Shh," he answered, and like the rest of this conversation, he sounded rough and angry.

Mason was a lot taller than she was, at least six foot three, so Abbie came up on her toes to look over his shoulder. She saw nothing. Just the darkness and the trees. Still, that nothing got her heart racing.

Because someone had set that fire.

In her attempts to evade Mason, Abbie had failed to realize that if Mason wasn't on to her, if he didn't know why she'd really come to the ranch, then someone else had set that fire.

Someone else had tried to scare her. Or worse.

Hurt her.

"You think someone's out there?" she asked.

But Mason only issued another *shh* and looked around as if he expected them to be ambushed at any moment.

Abbie stayed on her toes, although the arches of her feet were cramping. She ignored the pain and watched.

She didn't have to watch long.

There.

In the center of that tree cluster. She saw the movement. So slight that at first she thought maybe it was a shadow created by the low-hanging branches swaying in the wind. But then, the shadow ducked out of sight.

"I'm Deputy Mason Ryland," Mason shouted. "Identify yourself."

Silence. Well, except for her own heartbeat drumming in her ears. Who was out there? The person who'd set the fire? Or was this something worse?

"Get down on the ground," Mason said to her. "I'm going closer."

Abbie wanted to shout no, that it could be too dangerous to do that, but Mason caught onto her arm and pushed her to the ground. "Stay put," he warned. And he started in the direction of those trees.

With each step he took, her heart pounded harder, so hard that Abbie thought it might crack her ribs. But she didn't move, didn't dare do anything that might distract Mason.

He kept his gun aimed. Ready. Kept his focus on the trees. When he was about fifteen yards away, there was more movement. Abbie got a better look then—at the person dressed head to toe in black.

Including the gun.

The moonlight flickered off the silver barrel.

"Watch out!" Abbie yelled to Mason.

But it was too late. The person in black pointed the gun right at Mason.

Chapter Three

Mason dived to the ground and hoped Abbie had done the same. He braced himself for the shot.

It came all right.

The bullet blasted through the night air, the sound tearing through him. Mason took aim and returned fire. The gunman ducked just in time, and Mason's shot slammed into the tree and sent a spray of splinters everywhere.

And that's when it hit Mason. The gunman hadn't fired at him.

But at Abbie.

Mason glanced over his shoulder to make sure she was okay. She seemed to be. She had stayed put on the ground with her hands covering her head. Good. But her hands wouldn't stop a bullet.

What the devil was going on?

First the fire, now this. It wasn't the first time danger had come to the ranch, but it was a first attack on one of his employees.

An employee who had plenty of questions to answer.

After Mason took care of this gunman, he would ask Abbie those questions. First, he wanted this shooter alive to answer some, too, but he had no trouble taking this guy out if it came down to it.

Mason kept watch on the spot where he'd last seen the

gunman, and he lifted his head slightly so he could have a better chance of hearing any kind of movement. He heard some all right.

Footsteps.

Mason cursed. The gunman was running.

Escaping.

Mason fired another shot into the trees and hoped it would cause the guy to stop. It didn't. Once the sound of the blast cleared, Mason heard the footsteps again and knew the shooter was headed for the fence. He would make it there, too, because it wasn't that far away, and once he scaled it, he could disappear into the woods.

That wouldn't give Mason those answers he wanted.

Mason got to a crouching position and watched the fence, hoping that he would be able to see the shooter and wound him enough to make him stop. But when the sound of the footsteps stopped, the guy was nowhere in sight.

"Don't get up," Mason barked to Abbie.

But that's exactly what *he* did. He kept his gun ready, but he started running and made a beeline to the fence. Mason ran as fast as he could. However, it wasn't fast enough. He heard the gunman drop to the other side of the fence.

Mason considered climbing the fence and going after him. That's what the rancher in him wanted to do anyway. But his cop's training and instincts reminded him that that would be a quick way to get himself killed.

Maybe Abbie, too.

The gunman could be there waiting for Mason to appear and could shoot him, and then go after Abbie. His brothers and some of the ranch hands were no doubt on the way to help, but they might not arrive in time to save her.

So Mason waited and stewed. Whoever had set that fire and shot at Abbie would pay for this.

When he was certain they weren't about to be gunned down, Mason stood. He kept his attention and gun on the fence and backed his way to Abbie.

"Let's get out of here," he ordered.

Mason didn't have to tell her twice. She sprang to her bare feet and started toward the ranch—backward, as Mason was doing.

"Why did he try to kill you?" he asked her without taking his attention off the fence.

Abbie didn't jump to deny it, but she didn't volunteer anything either. She was definitely hesitating, and Mason didn't like that.

"Why?" he pressed.

"I'm in the Federal Witness Protection Program," she finally said.

Of all the things Mason had expected to hear, that wasn't on his list. But his list now included a whole barnyard of questions.

"Who's the gunman?" he asked.

She shook her head. "I don't know."

Mason couldn't help it. He cursed again. "And you thought it was okay to bring this kind of danger to the ranch without warning anyone? Someone other than you could have been killed tonight."

He knew that sounded gruff. Insensitive even. But no one had ever accused him of putting sensitivity first. Still, he felt…something. Something he cursed, too. Because Mason hated the fear in Abbie's voice. Hated even more the vulnerability he saw in her eyes.

Oh, man.

This was a damsel-in-distress reaction. He could face down a cold-blooded killer and not flinch. But a woman in pain was something he had a hard time stomaching. Especially this woman.

He blamed that on the flimsy gown. And cursed again.

"I need details," he demanded. "Why are you in witness protection, and why would someone want you dead?"

She opened her mouth to answer, but before she could say anything, Mason heard Grayson call out to them. "Are you two okay?"

Mason was, but Abbie looked ready to keel over. "We're not hurt," he shouted to his brother. Because the gunman was probably long gone, Mason turned in Grayson's direction so he could get to him faster. "The guy shot at Abbie."

"Abbie?" Grayson questioned. Like the other half dozen or so ranch hands with him, he was armed.

"She's the new cutting-horse trainer I hired," Mason explained. "And she's in witness protection."

The news seemed to surprise Grayson as much as it had him.

"I don't know who tried to kill me," Abbie volunteered.

Her voice wasn't just shaky, it was all breath and nerves. She let out a small yelp when she stumbled. Probably landed on a rock, because there were plenty enough to step on. That did it. Mason put his gun in the back waist of his jeans and scooped her up. He didn't forget that it was the second time tonight he'd had her in his arms—and neither circumstance had been very good.

Too bad *she* felt good.

She smelled good, too, even though he could pick up traces of the smoke. Her scent, the feel of her, stirred things he had no intentions of feeling, so he told those feelings to back off. Way off. He wasn't going there with Abbie.

Then he looked down at her. Saw the shiny tears in her eyes. Heard the slight hitch in her breath when she tried to choke back those tears.

"I've been in witness protection for twenty-one years," she whispered.

Mason did the math. If he remembered correctly, Abbie was thirty-two. That meant she'd entered the program at age eleven. A kid.

"And nothing like this has ever happened to you?" Grayson asked, sounding a little too much like a hard-nosed cop for Mason's liking.

That was a big red flag, because Mason remembered that it was a question he should have asked. No. He should have *demanded*. He forced himself to remember that he was a deputy sheriff and that Abbie had put them all in danger.

Still, he felt that twinge of something he rarely felt. Or rarely acknowledged anyway.

Sympathy.

He'd rather feel actual pain.

"Years ago, someone tried to kill me," Abbie answered. And she paused for a long time. "Not long after my mom and I entered witness protection, someone fired shots at me." Another pause. "They killed my mother."

Oh, hell.

Nothing could have stopped that slam of sympathy. *Nothing.*

Mason and his brother exchanged glances, and Mason knew there'd be more questions. Had to be. Grayson would need to investigate the fire and shooting. One of them would also need to contact the U.S. Marshals who ran witness protection and let them know that Abbie's identity had been compromised.

Still, twenty-one years was a long time to go without a *compromise*. And Mason considered something else. Why had it happened now, only three days after Abbie had arrived at the Ryland ranch?

A coincidence?

His gut was telling him no.

Mason kept that to himself and trudged the last leg of the distance to the ranch. He headed straight for his office, and this time he didn't intend to let Abbie run away.

The first thing Mason did was place her on the sofa again, and despite all the sympathy he was feeling, he gave her a warning glance to stay put. Grayson followed him inside, no doubt ready to question Abbie, but Mason didn't plan to start until he'd located a few things. First, he got Abbie a blanket and then he found her some socks.

"Who killed your mother?" Grayson started. "And why?"

Abbie put on the socks, mumbled a thanks and pulled the blanket around her.

Her sigh was long and weary. "My mother and I went into witness protection after she testified against her boss, Vernon Ferguson, a corrupt San Antonio cop." Her voice was as shaky as the rest of her. "Ferguson got off on a technicality, and shortly afterward he sent a hired gun named Hank Tinsley after us. Tinsley turned up dead a few days later."

Mason figured there were plenty of details to go along with that sterile explanation. The stuff of nightmares. Something he knew a little about because his grandfather Chet had been shot and left to die. Mason had been seventeen, and even though nearly twenty-one years had passed, the wound still felt fresh and raw.

Always would.

Not just for him but for all his brothers.

That wound had deepened to something incapable of being healed when his father had left just weeks later. And then his mother had committed suicide.

Oh, yeah. He could sympathize with Abbie.

But sympathy wasn't going to keep her safe.

"You think this Vernon Ferguson came after you to-night?" Mason asked. He stood over her, side by side with Grayson.

Abbie shook her head. "Maybe."

It was a puzzling answer, and Grayson jumped on it. "You have somebody else other than Ferguson trying to kill you?"

"I don't know. Over the past twenty years, Ferguson has managed to find me two other times, and both times he sent hired guns. Nothing recent, though. Mainly because we've been very careful."

Mason didn't miss the *we,* and later he would ask who this person was in her life. Because it might be important to the investigation. Not because he was thinking she had a boyfriend stashed away. On her job application she had said she was single, but that didn't mean she wasn't in love with someone.

And for some reason, a reason Mason didn't want to consider, that riled him a little.

Abbie closed her eyes a moment and when she opened her eyes, she turned them on Mason. "My caseworker is Deputy U.S. Marshal Harlan McKinney over in Maverick County. He'll need to know about this."

Mason nodded, but it was Grayson who reacted. "I'll call him. And check in with the fire chief." Grayson glanced at her shoeless feet peeking out from the blanket. "I'll also ask my wife about getting you some clothes."

"Thank you," she said in a whisper. Abbie didn't move until Grayson was out of the office and had shut the door. Then she sat up as if ready to leave.

"You're not going anywhere," Mason reminded her.

She blinked. "But I figured you'd demand that I leave. It's not safe for any of you with me here."

"That's probably true, but you're still not going anywhere." In case she'd forgotten, he took his badge from his desk and clipped it to the waist of his jeans. "You've got six lawmen on this ranch."

Her gaze came to his again. "And yet someone still got to me."

Yeah, and that meant whoever had done this was as bold as brass, stupid or desperate. Mason didn't like any of those scenarios.

"Why would Ferguson still want you dead if he got off on the charges with a technicality?" Mason asked. He located a black T-shirt in the closet and pulled it on. He grabbed his black Stetson, too.

"Maybe he still considers me a loose end." But she didn't sound convinced.

And that only reinforced the fact that something just wasn't right here.

Mason pulled his chair over to the sofa and sat so that he'd be more at her eye level. Abbie adjusted her position, too, easing away from him, and in the process the blanket slid off her.

Great.

He felt another punch of, well, something stirring below the belt when he got another look at the gown. And at her breasts barely concealed beneath the fabric. Not a good combination with that vulnerable face and her honey-brown eyes.

"I swear, I didn't mean for this to happen," she said. "I didn't know Ferguson could find me. I've always been careful."

Mason made a heavy sigh and reached out. He doubted his touch would give her much comfort, but he had to do something. He put his fingertips against her arm. Rubbed gently.

And he felt that blasted below-the-belt pull happen again.

Their gazes met, and the corner of her mouth lifted. Not a smile but more of a baffled expression. Either she figured out he was going nuts or else she was feeling something, too.

"For the record, I didn't think you'd be like this," she said.

The cryptic remark got his attention, and Mason would have asked what she meant. If her gown hadn't shifted. Yeah, he saw her breasts. The tops of them anyway. And while they snagged his attention in a bad way, it was what was between her breasts that snagged it even more.

The pendant.

Or rather, the silver concho.

He instantly recognized it because he had one just like it. All of his brothers did. A custom-made gift from their father with their initials on the back. A blood gift he'd given them all just days before he'd run out on them.

Abbie gasped when she followed Mason's gaze, and she slapped her hand over the concho. Mason just shoved her hand away and had a better look at the front of it.

And there it was.

The back-to-back *R*s for the Ryland ranch. This wasn't a new piece either. It was weathered and battered, showing every day of its twenty-one years.

Abbie tried again to push his hand away, but Mason grabbed both her wrists. He turned the concho over, even though it meant touching her breasts. But it wasn't her breasts that held his attention right now. It was the other initials on the back.

B.R.

For his father, Boone Ryland.

Mason let go of the concho, leaned down and got right

in Abbie's face, but it took him a moment to get his teeth unclenched so he could ask her the mother of all questions.

"Who the hell are you?"

Chapter Four

Abbie knew her situation had just gone from bad to worse. She also knew that Mason wasn't just going to let her run out of there again. Not that she could.

Not now.

Not after the gunman's attack.

She'd opened this dangerous Pandora's box and had to stay around long enough to close it. If she could. But closing it meant first answering the Texas-sized question that Mason had just asked.

Who the hell are you?

"I'm Abbie Baker," she said, knowing that didn't clarify anything, especially because it was a name given to her twenty-one years ago by the U.S. Marshals when she and her mom had entered witness protection.

Her real name was Madelyn Turner. Maddie. But she no longer thought of herself as that little girl who'd nearly died from a hired gun's bullet.

She was Abbie Baker now.

And she had a thoroughly riled, confused cowboy lawman looming over her. He was waiting for answers that didn't involve her real name or anything else so mundane. Mason's attention and narrowed glare were on the concho.

"Where did you get it?" he asked.

Abbie considered another lie. She'd gotten so good at

them over the years, but no one was *that* good. There was no way she could convince Mason that she'd found the concho and then had coincidentally applied for a job at the Ryland ranch.

There was nothing chance about it, and now she might have endangered not just Mason but also his entire family. Someone had come after her tonight, and she had to get to the bottom of that—fast.

First, though, she had to get past Mason, literally. And that meant giving him enough information to satisfy him but not so much that he would have a major meltdown.

"Where did you get the concho?" he repeated.

Abbie tried not to look as frightened as she felt, but she figured she wasn't very successful. "Your father gave it to me."

She saw the surprise go through his eyes. Maybe Mason had thought she'd stolen it or something.

"My *father?*" he snapped.

Abbie settled for a nod, knowing she would have to add details. But the devil was in those details, and once Mason heard them, he might physically toss her off the ranch. That couldn't happen at this exact moment.

"When?" he pressed. "Why?"

She had no choice but to clear her throat so she could answer. "When I turned sixteen. He said it was a good-luck charm."

That was a lie. Actually, Boone had said he wanted her to have it because it was his most valuable possession. Something he'd reserved for his own children.

Nothing about his severe expression changed. Mason's wintry eyes stayed narrowed to slits. His jaw muscles stirred. He continued to glare at her. For several snail-crawling seconds anyway. Then he cursed. One really bad word. Before he turned and scrubbed his hands over his face. It seemed to take him another couple of moments to get his jaw unclenched.

"So Boone is alive," he mumbled. "Or at least he was when you were sixteen."

"He still is alive," Abbie confirmed. "I talked to him on the phone before I went to bed." She chose her words carefully. "He met my mother and me about four months before she was killed."

"Where?" he barked.

"Maverick County. But we've lived plenty of other places since then." She paused because she had to gather her breath. "We move a lot, finding work at ranches all over the Southwest. He's always worried that Vernon Ferguson will find me." And finish what he'd started.

Mason's eyes narrowed even more. "Boone lived with you?"

"He raised me," Abbie corrected.

That didn't improve Mason's ornery mood. More profanity, and the corner of his mouth lifted in a dry smile that held no humor at all.

"He raised you." And he repeated it. "He couldn't raise his own sons or be a husband to his wife, but yet he took you in. Why?"

Abbie had asked herself that a thousand times and still didn't have the answer. "It was either that or I would have had to go into foster care. There weren't many options for a kid in witness protection."

"You would have been better off in foster care," Mason mumbled. "I figured the SOB was dead." He held up his hand in a stop gesture when she started to speak. "He should be dead."

That sent a chill through her. That chill got significantly worse when Mason grabbed her arm and pulled her to her feet.

"He sent you here," Mason accused. "Why? He wants to mend fences with us after all these years?"

Abbie didn't get a chance to deny it.

His grip was hard and punishing. "Well, you can just go back to Maverick County and tell the bastard that he's not welcome here. Neither is his lackey. Consider yourself officially fired."

"He didn't send me," Abbie managed to say.

Mason no doubt heard her, but he didn't respond except to haul her toward the door. Abbie dug in her heels. Or rather, tried. It was like wrestling with an angry bear. She wasn't a weakling, and her work with the cutting horses had honed some muscles that most women didn't have, but she was no physical match for the likes of Mason.

Still, she had to make him understand.

"Boone didn't send me," she repeated. "In fact, he wouldn't be happy if he knew I was here." And that was a massive understatement.

That stopped Mason, finally, even though they were just inches from the door.

"Boone knows how much you hate him," she added.

Oh, that put some fire into those ice-gray eyes. "He can't begin to imagine how much I hate him." His attention dropped back to the concho. "I put a bullet through mine and then nailed it to my bedroom wall so it's the first thing I see when I wake up. That way, I can remember that the man who fathered me is a worthless piece of dirt."

Abbie had expected anger, but she hadn't quite braced herself enough for this outright rage. Boone had been right. He had done the unforgivable when he'd walked out on his family. At least it was unforgivable in Mason's eyes, and she wondered if she stood a better chance pleading her case to one of his brothers. The problem was, she might not get the chance to do that.

Mason started moving again, toward the door.

"Why did Boone leave Silver Creek?" she asked.

Again, that stopped him. Well, sort of. Mason didn't open the door, but he put her back right against it, and he kept his grip hard and tight on her shoulders. She was trapped, and Boone's warning came flying through her head.

Mason isn't the forgive-or-forget sort.

It was one of the few times Boone had talked about his sons, about the life he'd left behind here in Silver Creek. Boone wouldn't have wanted her to come here, but she'd had no choice. This was her best bet at finding the answers to why Boone had been so secretive lately. He was definitely keeping something from her, and Abbie was scared that the *something* meant he was in serious danger.

"You tell me why he ran off," Mason challenged.

She shook her head. Actually, her whole body was shaking, maybe from the adrenaline. Maybe the cold.

Maybe Mason.

She glanced down between them, at the fact that their bodies were pressed against each other. Not good. After all, despite the anger and Boone's warning about this particular Ryland, Mason was a man, and she was a woman.

Mason must have realized it, too, because while still scowling and cursing, he stepped back. "Why did Boone leave?" he repeated.

Abbie had to shake her head again. "I don't know." It was the truth, but she wished she had the answer because it would no doubt clear up a lot of other questions she had. "He wouldn't say. But for what it's worth, he was a good surrogate father to me."

Mason made a skeptical sound and threw open the door. However, he didn't toss her out. That's because his oldest brother, Grayson, was standing in the way. He had an armful of clothes, a concerned look on his face and the same cop's eyes as Mason. And he eyed the grip that Mason had on her.

"A problem?" Grayson asked, suspicion dripping from his voice. He waited until Mason let go of her before he handed her the clothes from his wife.

"Yeah, there's a problem," Mason verified. "Boone sent her."

"He didn't," Abbie answered as fast as she could, and she was getting darn tired of that broken-record accusation.

Grayson looked first at Mason. Then her. "Is that why you're here at the ranch, because of Boone?"

"No," Abbie said at the exact moment that Mason said, "Yes."

Grayson gave them a raised eyebrow. "Well, which is it?"

Both Rylands stared at her, waiting. "Boone doesn't know I'm here, and he didn't send me," Abbie insisted. "He believes he doesn't stand a chance of reconciling with any of you."

"He's right," Mason jumped to answer.

Grayson didn't voice an opinion, but his expression made it clear that Mason and he were of a like mind. And that meant Abbie was wasting her time and putting them in future danger for no reason. Well, except that she might get some answers from Grayson that she hadn't managed to get from his brother.

Abbie hugged the clothes to her chest and looked Grayson in the eyes. "Boone never talked much about all of you, so I don't know why he left."

Mason cursed.

Grayson lifted his shoulder. "Does it matter why?" he asked.

Unlike Mason, he actually waited for her to answer. "Maybe." That required a deep breath. "Something's wrong."

"If he's dying, then you'd better break the news to someone who gives a flying fig," Mason grumbled.

Abbie was about to tell him that Boone wasn't dying, but she had no idea if that was true. And that made her sick to her stomach. Yes, Mason had a right to be this enraged, but she was already getting tired of it. He was aiming that venom not just at her but also at the man who'd raised her. A man she loved like a father.

"Get dressed," Mason said again. This time it was an order, and he grabbed on to the concho and shoved it back into her gown so that it was out of sight. "I'll drive you into town so you can leave Silver Creek."

Grayson had a different reaction. He flexed those previously raised eyebrows. "Someone just tried to kill her," he reminded Mason. "And that someone likely set fire to the guesthouse with her in it. As the sheriff, I think I'd like to get to the bottom of that first before she leaves."

"Boone sent her," Mason argued.

"And we can send her back. After the doc checks her out and she answers a few questions." Because Mason was clearly gearing up for an argument, Grayson tipped his head to the clothes. "Go ahead and change."

Abbie considered staying put, considered trying to convince them that she wasn't there on a mission of peacemaking, but it was obviously an argument she'd lose. On a huff she headed to the bathroom but didn't shut the door all the way. She needed to hear what the Ryland brothers were planning to do with her. Too bad she couldn't quite manage that because both lowered their voices to whispers.

Angry ones.

Mason was still no doubt insisting that she leave immediately. Grayson had the more level head, and she remembered Boone calling him an old soul.

Abbie hurriedly changed into loose pants and oversized denim shirt. No underwear, but the flat slipper-type shoes fit. She was ready to face down the enemy, or rather her former employer, until she caught sight of herself in the mirror. Mercy. There was soot on her face. Her hair was a tangled mess, and there were dark circles under her eyes. And then she wondered why she cared.

Oh, yes. She remembered.

Mason, and that body-to-body contact. Abbie cursed him. Cursed herself. She didn't let men get under her skin, and she wasn't about to start now.

Steeled with that reminder, Abbie walked back into the main room, only to have both Ryland men stop their whispered conversation and stare at her.

"So, what's the verdict?" she came right out and asked. Of course, Mason scowled at her and mumbled something she probably didn't want to hear anyway.

"Our other brothers Dade and Nate are out looking for the man who took shots at you," Grayson informed her. He was all cop now. "Any idea who he was?"

She shook her head. "It was too dark to see his face."

Mason swung his attention in her direction. "What about the man who set the fire? Too dark to see him, too?"

Abbie ignored the skeptical, snarky tone. "I didn't see him," she verified. "In fact, I didn't see anyone. I only sensed someone was there."

"Your senses are good," Grayson volunteered. "Because I looked at the door that Mason pulled off you. It'd been torn from its hinges. If you didn't do that—"

"I didn't."

Grayson lifted his shoulder. "Then someone else did. I'm guessing it was the same man who fired those shots."

She guessed the same. Abbie also guessed that his brothers would give it their best efforts in searching for the man. But she also knew there were miles and miles of wooded area surrounding the Ryland ranch. The odds weren't good. And that put a hard knot back in her stomach.

"He'll be back," she said before she could stop herself. Abbie instantly regretted the admission, but it didn't surprise Grayson. Perhaps not Mason either. It was hard to tell because his face seemed to be frozen in that permanent glare.

"Boone didn't send me," she reiterated. "And I'm sorry that you're riled because someone tried to kill me on *your* ranch."

"I'm not riled because of that." That got rid of the glare. Judging from his annoyed huff, Mason hadn't intended to ditch the glare, raise his voice. Or show even a smidgen of what had to be a bad temper to go along with that gruff exterior.

But Abbie hadn't intended to go the snark route either. "Look, I'm frustrated. Scared. And feeling a dozen other things that you clearly don't want me to feel. I'm sorry."

"Quit apologizing," Mason snapped. He stared at her. And stared. Then cursed again. "Quit apologizing," he repeated.

Like the little arm rub he'd given her earlier, before he'd seen the concho, it sounded, well, human.

Grayson gave them both a stern glance, especially his brother. "Are you two sleeping together or something?"

"No!" Mason and she said in unison. Mason shot his brother a look that could have frozen Hades.

Grayson did some more staring and then made a sound of disbelief. "Then maybe we can concentrate on finding the man who tried to kill you." He waited until he had their attention before he continued. "I've already made a call to Marshal Harlan McKinney to let him know what's going on, and I've put out feelers to find out if Vernon Ferguson's connected to this."

She gave a weary sigh and pushed her hair from her face. "You won't find a connection," Abbie assured him. "Ferguson's too smart for that." And that reminder caused her to go still. "Ferguson found me awfully fast. I've been here at the ranch only three days."

"Maybe Boone told him," Mason instantly suggested.

Abbie didn't even have to consider it. "Boone doesn't know I'm here. That's the truth. I told him I was visiting a friend in Austin."

Mason gave her a flat stare. "So you're telling us the truth, but you lied to him?"

"Yes." She ignored his sarcasm and turned toward Mason. "Did you do some kind of background check on me?"

Mason probably would have preferred to continue the sniping match, but she saw the moment that he turned from an angry son to a concerned rancher and lawman. "Of course. I use a P.I. agency in San Antonio to screen potential employees." He paused. "I don't have the report back on you yet."

Later, she would curse herself for not realizing that Mason would run such a check. She didn't have an arrest record. In fact, not many records at all, and that would have perhaps flagged a P.I.'s interest.

It had probably flagged Marshal McKinney, too, but Abbie had called him right before she applied for the job at the ranch to tell him she might be working there for a short period of time. She'd also asked the marshal not to tell Boone, and McKinney must have complied because

Boone hadn't tried to stop her. And he would have if he'd known she was anywhere near Silver Creek.

Abbie shook her head and stared at Mason. "So why did you hire me before you got the report?"

"Because he needed a cutter," Grayson jumped to answer. "He goes through five or six cutting-horse trainers a year."

The muscles in Mason's jaw tightened. "Because most aren't worth spit." Another pause, and he tipped his head toward her. "She seemed to know what she was doing."

"Thanks. Your father trained me," she added, knowing it would cause his glare to return. It did. Not just from Mason, but his brother, too.

She huffed but regretted that little jab. It was clear she wasn't going to win them over to her side, so it was best to tell them the truth and hope they'd be willing to do something to help her.

Abbie took a deep breath before she started. "Something happened about a month ago. I'm not sure what," she added because it looked as if both Rylands were about to interrupt her. "I know it started when Boone heard the news reports about the senator who committed suicide here in Silver Creek."

"Ford Herrington," Grayson supplied.

Abbie waited for them to add more. They didn't. But she'd done her own reading about the senator. He'd confessed to murdering his wife and the Ryland sons' grandfather Chet McLaurin, before taking his own life.

"What connection did Boone have to Senator Herrington?" Abbie asked.

"You mean other than Herrington murdering Boone's father-in-law?" Mason asked. He was back to being a cowboy cop again.

She nodded. "Is there something more?"

Mason shook his head, huffed. "According to Ford, our grandfather was having an affair with Ford's wife."

"Was he?" she pressed, though she still couldn't see the connection with Boone.

"Maybe." And when Mason paused, Grayson took up the explanation. "His wife was having an affair with someone. Ford's daughter, Lynette, confirmed that. She overheard her mother talking about it before she was killed, and Lynette has no reason to lie, because she's our sister-in-law."

So maybe that was the connection she'd been searching for. But why would a decades-old affair between a senator's wife and Boone's father-in-law have such an impact now? Especially because everyone seemed to know about it.

"Is it possible that the senator's wife got pregnant and had your grandfather's baby?" Yes, she was grasping at straws, but she had to find what had set all of this in motion.

Mason lifted his shoulder. "I suppose she could have gotten pregnant, but she didn't give birth. No time for that. From the time line we've been able to come up with, Ford killed her only about a month after the affair started."

Well, there went her secret-baby theory.

"Boone got upset when he saw the news reports about the senator's suicide," she added. "And he followed the story like a hawk. I'd never seen him like that, and since then he's been secretive. Agitated. He even hired a P.I., and he won't tell me why."

The brothers exchanged concerned glances. "What's your theory?"

Abbie had to take a deep breath. "I suspect something bad happened to Boone all those years ago. Something bad enough to cause him to walk out on his family."

"And what would that be?" Mason's tone wasn't quite as lawmanlike as it had been for his other questions. The emotion and old pain were seeping through.

"I'm not sure," Abbie admitted. "But a week ago I heard him talking to someone on the phone. I don't know who, but it could have been the P.I. I only caught pieces of the conversation, but Boone mentioned the ranch. And all of you."

"Us?" Mason challenged.

She nodded. "I think he was worried about your safety." Mercy, she wished she'd heard more of that call. "He also said something else."

"What?" Mason pressed when she paused.

Abbie tried to repeat this part verbatim. "Boone said the past was catching up with him and that it wouldn't be long before someone came to kill him."

Chapter Five

Mason listened to every word that Abbie said, but it took a moment for her bombshell to sink in.

"Who wants Boone dead?" Mason asked. "Other than me, that is."

There was a flash of annoyance in her eyes. Probably because she felt he was being too hard on her surrogate daddy. He wasn't. There wasn't such a thing as too hard when it came to Boone Ryland.

"I don't know who wants him dead," she insisted. "But I could tell from his voice and body language that the threat was real."

Hell. This was not a turn that Mason wanted. It might not even be true, but just the fact that Abbie had tossed it out there meant it would have be investigated. Not by him. Well, not unless he learned that Boone had been the one to cause the fire and the gunman.

Then Boone would have to *answer* for it.

Grayson shook his head. "If Boone thought someone was trying to kill him, why would he let you out of his sight?"

It was a good question, especially considering Boone had chosen to raise this woman and she seemingly had such a high opinion of him. Mason only wished he'd thought of the question first. He couldn't let the past and Abbie's vulnerable eyes cloud his head.

Too late, the little voice inside him mumbled.

Mason would make it his mission to prove that little voice wrong.

"Like I said, I lied to him," Abbie explained. "Boone thought it would be a good idea if I disappeared for a while and put some distance between him and me. He wouldn't say why," she quickly added. "He seemed relieved when I told him I was going to Austin for a month, but I didn't dare tell him I was coming here, or he would have tried to stop me. He knows none of you want contact with him, directly or otherwise. I just wanted to find out why he might be in danger."

So if Abbie was telling the truth, and Mason thought she might be—about this anyway—then Boone was in some kind of danger and he didn't want that spilling onto her. Clearly, he loved his foster daughter a heck of a lot more than he'd loved his sons.

But that didn't surprise Mason.

"I need to do some checking," Grayson finally said. "If the fire and the gunman are connected to Boone, then I'll have to ask him some questions."

Mason waited for Abbie to object. She didn't. Strange. Mason had thought she might try to come up with a good reason why Grayson shouldn't do that. Mason was certainly trying to come up with one. He didn't want Grayson or anyone else in the family to have any contact with the man.

However, the alternative to questioning Boone wasn't a good one: the possibility of continued danger and threats on the ranch.

Grayson looked at him. "I need to wrap up some things with the fire chief and check on Nate and Dade."

Good plan, but Mason knew if his brothers had found the gunman, they would have called.

"Why don't you go ahead and take Abbie to the main house? The doctor will be here soon," Grayson suggested. Mason wasn't sure what Grayson saw in his expression, but it caused him to add, "She's just the messenger, Mason. She didn't cause Boone to walk out on us all those years ago."

Abbie looked both uncomfortable with that reminder and a little relieved. Of course, if she was telling the truth about all of this, she would no doubt want them to leap headfirst into saving Boone.

That wasn't going to happen.

Unless…saving his sorry butt would mean keeping the family safe. But Mason was a long way from believing that.

"Come on," Mason told Abbie, and he started out of his office and toward the main house. He kept his gun ready, just in case, but he doubted the gunman would make a re-peat appearance tonight.

"You think this is a smart move?" Abbie asked, catch-ing up with him. "I don't want the gunman coming to the house."

"Neither do I," Mason assured her. "It's the safest place on the ranch. It has a security system with surveillance cameras."

And some areas of the grounds had cameras, too. As soon as he had Abbie tucked away in one of the guest rooms, she could wait for the doctor and he'd check the surveillance feed to see what he could find out about the gunman.

About Abbie, too.

"Your family isn't going to like my being there," she mumbled. She followed him along the crushed-limestone walking path that would take them directly to the back porch.

Mason couldn't disagree with that. They wouldn't like it. But they wouldn't turn her out. Not tonight anyway. If he found out she'd told him another lie, even a single one, then he would toss her out himself.

"I didn't mean for any of this to happen," Abbie added. "I figured I'd come here, get some answers to save Boone and then leave."

"Guess you figured wrong, huh?"

But Mason immediately regretted that dig. Yeah, they'd been jabbing at each other since she'd spilled the beans about Boone, but it wasn't helping matters. There was no way Abbie could ever understand how Boone had ripped his sons to pieces and then turned his back on them. And that led him back full circle to a question he just had to ask.

"Boone knew about my mother's suicide?"

There was enough illumination from the security lights and the house that Mason could see the answer on Abbie's suddenly stark face. "He knew. He didn't talk about it, but I heard him mention it once to my mother."

Her mother. Probably the woman Boone had bedded down with while still a married man. Mason didn't intend to ask about that or anything else that wasn't directly relevant to the investigation into the fire and gunman. The less he knew about Boone, the better. The man was like battery acid, eating away at the people he'd once claimed to love.

"I think Boone kept up with all of you as best he could," she continued. "But he always did it in a way not to draw attention to himself."

Yeah, so that no one could find him after he'd run out.

But something about that didn't sit right. Not now, not after meeting Abbie. Maybe Boone had lain low for her sake. To keep the corrupt ex-cop, Ferguson, from finding her.

More battery acid.

Boone had protected Abbie, but he hadn't cared a rat's you-know-what about his own blood kin for the past two decades.

Mason walked ahead of her onto the porch and punched in the code to unlock the door. Yet another recently added security measure. After a couple of intruders and even attacks on the grounds, Mason had taken a lot of measures that he hoped would keep everyone safe.

When he stepped into the kitchen ahead of Abbie, Mason slid his gun into the waist of his jeans, but he nearly drew it again when he heard the movement.

"It's just me," his kid brother Kade greeted. "Grayson called, said there was a problem, so I turned off the lights."

Mason kept them off, but he could still see because of the outside lights. Kade was at the table feeding a bottle to one of his twin girls. Mason didn't have a clue which one because Leah and Mia were identical.

"Everything okay?" Kade asked. "Did they find the gunman?"

"Not yet." When Abbie didn't come inside, Mason took her arm again and urged her in. Best to minimize her time outside because the gunman was still at large.

Kade's attention landed on Abbie. "It's true? She's been with Boone all these years?"

"Pretty much." Well, unless she was lying, but Mason couldn't think of a good reason for her to do that—yet. Still it didn't make sense to lie about something that was going to make her an outcast.

And that's exactly what it had done.

Kade didn't sound any happier about this situation than Mason was.

"I'm sorry for all the trouble," Abbie mumbled. She inched closer when Kade put the baby against his chest to burp her. Even in the dim light, Mason could see Abbie smile at the infant. "How many grandchildren does Boone have?"

Mason wanted to answer *none* because the man would have to be a father first before he became a grandfather. Boone wasn't anywhere close to being a father.

"Six," Kade answered, still staring at her.

Abbie's smile dissolved, probably because of Kade's less-than-warm tone. That was Mason's cue to get her out of there.

"This way," Mason instructed, and he led her out of the kitchen, into the foyer and up the stairs. It wasn't a short walk. The three-story house was huge, and it was getting bigger now that Kade and his wife were building another addition so they'd have private quarters.

He heard Abbie's breath racing by the time they made it to the top of the stairs. She was winded, he was betting. This was part of the adrenaline crash. Soon, she'd be too exhausted to stand.

Mason led her to the room directly across from his. Part of him wanted to put her as far away as possible, but the danger wasn't over. Plus, he wasn't sure he could trust her. He didn't want her sneaking out before they got the answers needed for their investigation.

"The guest room," he let her know, throwing open the door. "The doctor will be here soon to make sure you're okay. If you need anything, I'll be in there." He pointed to his own suite.

She nodded, pushed her hair from her face, but she didn't go inside. "In the morning I'll need to go to the bank so I can get some money to leave. All my cash burned in the guesthouse, and I don't have a credit card."

Mason hadn't forgotten about the fire, but for the first time he realized all of Abbie's belongings had been inside. "I owe you some wages, and if it's not enough, I'll lend you the money."

She managed another of those awkward smiles. "You're really anxious to get me out of here."

"Can you blame me?"

"No." She shook her head.

Mason didn't miss the slight tremble in her voice. She was trembling again, too. "You think it's safe for you to go?"

"It's never safe." Her gaze came back to his. "If I don't get a chance to tell you tomorrow, thank you for saving me not once but twice. And for hiring me. I'm thirty-two, but it's the first time I've gotten a job without Boone's help."

For some reason that admission and the trembling bothered him. "You don't need his help for a job. I watched you with the horses yesterday, and you know what you're doing."

"That's high praise coming from you." She paused. "It wasn't a lie, you know. I really did read about the ranch, about what you've accomplished here. You've done a good job, Mason."

He didn't want to be flattered, but he was the ranch. It was his baby. He was as married to it as his brothers were to their spouses and badges. Yeah, he had a badge, too, but it would never mean as much as this place did.

"Good night," Abbie mumbled. She turned and stumbled right smack-dab into the door.

Mason automatically reached out and caught her. He didn't pull her into his arms or pick her up as he'd done before. The less contact, the better.

"You just need some rest," he assured her, but he didn't let go of her.

Abbie made a sound to indicate she didn't believe him. And with good reason. It was a lie. Unless she had nerves of steel, she was going to be dealing with the fire and attack for a while. The stuff of nightmares, which she'd no doubt have the moment she fell asleep.

When the trembling kept up, Mason mumbled some profanity, slipped his arm around her waist and led her to the bed. He didn't dawdle. Every moment he was next to Abbie like this was a moment of discomfort and only gave more thoughts of why he didn't want to think about the discomfort.

He deposited her on the bed, issued a hasty good-night and headed for the door.

Oh, man.

What the heck was going on inside his head? Except he was pretty sure his head wasn't in on these particular feelings. No. This was a behind-the-zipper, below-the-belt kind of reaction and a slap-in-the-face reminder that he really needed to take the time to be with a woman. *Soon.*

Not Abbie, of course.

She might put a strain on his Wranglers, but she was hands-off. There was no way he'd get past her association with Boone. Or the danger. The lies, too.

Hell, she had a whole state of strikes against her. No use spelling them all out again.

Mentally kicking himself, he headed to his room, took off his Stetson, slapped on the lights and made a beeline for his laptop in the sitting room–office area. Mostly office. There were files, memos and notes stacked high but neatly on the desk. Bessie's doing. He'd need to remember to thank the housekeeper-caregiver for digging out the place—again.

Once the laptop booted up, Mason sank down in the chair and clicked on the security camera icon. The images immediately popped onto the screen, and he saw the fire department still at work next to what was left of the guest cottage. Grayson was talking to Dade and Nate, which meant his brothers hadn't found the gunman.

Soon, Mason would get a call from one of them to let him know that and inform him of any other update on the search, but for now Mason tapped into the stored security feed, and he backtracked an hour.

No flames in the cottage then. No one lurking around either. But he kept watching, and he finally saw the shadowy figure near the back porch area. There were no security cameras there.

Had the guy known that?

Maybe. And it meant Mason had some modifications to make. He wanted that and all areas of the ranch covered even if it was too little, too late.

The person on the screen moved quickly, opening a gas can and dousing the porch with the liquid, but he didn't light it. He disappeared from sight. The seconds ticked away on the camera clock, a full minute passing before the front door of the cottage popped open. But it wasn't Abbie.

The arsonist again.

He'd obviously broken in or gone through the back to the front of the house. It was a man wearing dark clothes and a baseball cap slung low on his forehead. He had some kind of tool in his hand that he used to unhinge the door, and he propped it in place before he hurried back to the gas can. He lit it with the flick of a match.

Mason saw the flames burst around the back of the cottage, and he tried not to imagine Abbie being inside. She probably hadn't smelled the smoke at this point. Probably didn't know she was a thread away from dying.

The smoke and fire billowed from the cottage, and even though there was no audio, he saw the shadowy figure move behind a tree. He put away the tool that he'd used to unhinge the door and took something else from his pocket. Mason couldn't see what, but he copied the still frame and would send it for analysis.

Moments later on the screen, Mason saw Abbie throw open the door and yell for help. She was staggering, probably because of the smoke, and that was maybe why she hadn't realized the door was falling on her. She was too late to get out of the way. It slammed right into her back, knocking her to the ground.

Mason switched camera angles, going back to the arsonist. The guy stayed there behind the tree, watching and holding whatever was in his hand. He didn't budge until Mason came running toward the cottage and toward Abbie.

He didn't stay on that camera angle. Mason switched to the others, looking for the arsonist. Finally, he went to the camera near the fence.

Bingo.

The guy was hiding behind another tree. Waiting to gun down Abbie, no doubt. Mason zoomed in on his face, adjusting the feed until he captured the image. He copied it and immediately emailed it to his brother Gage at the Silver Creek sheriff's office. He also grabbed the phone and called him.

Gage answered on the first ring. "That's our intruder?" he asked Mason.

"He is. Can you run it through the facial recognition software? I also need to see if you can identify what he's holding in the first photo."

"Doing that now," Gage assured him, and Mason heard him typing something on the keyboard. "Everything else okay at the house?"

"The wives and kids are all safe, including your better

half." Mason waited for the rest of Gage's question. He didn't have to wait long.

"Boone's not trying to worm his way back into the family, is he?" Gage asked.

"I don't think so, but it doesn't matter. He's not stepping foot on this ranch."

"Good," Gage growled. He paused. "What about your horse trainer?"

"Abbie Baker," Mason provided. "She'll be leaving in the morning." And his Wranglers or his knee-jerk reaction to her situation weren't going to have a say in it.

"When Grayson called earlier, he said she believes someone wants to kill Boone," Gage went on. "*Get in line,* right?"

"Yeah." But the agreement didn't feel as right as Mason wanted it to feel. "She said something happened last month, that Boone started getting nervous."

Last month had significant meaning to Gage because Senator Ford Herrington, the man who'd murdered their grandfather, had also been Gage's father-in-law. And one month ago, Ford had committed suicide.

"Ford was as dirty as they came," Gage verified, "but he's dead. He's not a threat to any of us, including Boone."

Mason was about to agree with that as well, but Gage spoke before he could say anything. Well, he didn't speak, exactly.

Gage cursed.

"I got an immediate hit with the facial recognition software," Gage said. "We got some major trouble, brother. Lock up the ranch. I'll get there as fast as I can."

Chapter Six

Abbie eased open the guest room door and peered out into the hall. Empty.

Thank goodness.

She had no choice but to see Mason this morning so he could usher her off the ranch as fast as humanly possible, especially since the doctor had given her the all-clear when he'd examined her. But she hadn't wanted to run into any other Rylands. Not after the frosty reception she'd gotten from Grayson and Kade. It was clear she wasn't wanted here, and after the fire and the gunman, Abbie was ready to go home and regroup.

But she rethought that.

Maybe she shouldn't go back to Eagle Pass to the house that she shared with Boone. If by some chance the gunman managed to follow her, she could end up putting Boone in danger. She didn't want that. She'd already put enough people at risk, including herself, by trying to uncover a truth that Boone obviously didn't want her to.

Before Abbie could decide where she could go, she heard the sounds coming from Mason's room across the hall. Sounds she hadn't expected to hear.

Laughter.

The door to his suite was ajar, so Abbie went closer and had a peek inside. Mason was at his desk, a laptop and a breakfast tray positioned in front of him, but he wasn't alone. There was a red-haired toddler running circles around his desk, and each time the little girl reached his chair, Mason would goose her in the stomach. Both of them laughed with each round.

It was eavesdropping, plain and simple, but Abbie couldn't stop herself. She'd never seen this side of Mason. He certainly wasn't the gruff rancher or cowboy cop she'd encountered during her interview and her handful of workdays.

Abbie watched when the toddler smacked into the side of the desk and tumbled to the floor. No more laughter. She started to cry, and Mason sprang from his chair to pick her up. Abbie knew how it felt to be in his arms, and it had a similar soothing effect on the child. She stopped crying.

"Gotta be careful, Curly Locks," he said to her, and he brushed a kiss on her forehead. But the words had no sooner left his mouth, when his attention zoomed across the room and landed on Abbie.

"Are you coming in, or do you plan to stand out there all morning?" he asked.

Abbie felt her cheeks redden, and she hoped he hadn't realized just how long she'd been watching him. She stepped inside, Mason's gaze sliding over her from head to toe. She'd tried to look presentable in her borrowed clothes and with the toiletries she'd found in the bathroom. Abbie doubted that she did.

Mason, on the other hand, looked more than presentable in his well-worn jeans, black shirt and cowboy boots. Actually, he looked hot, something she wished she hadn't noticed. Worse, he no doubt noticed that she noticed.

Oh, mercy.

Focus, Abbie.

She was about to ask who would be driving her into Silver Creek, but Mason spoke before she could.

"This is Kimmie. Kimberly Ellen," he corrected, kissing the toddler's forehead again. "Her stepmom, Darcy, is hugging the toilet. Morning sickness. Her dad, Nate, is working. And the nannies are tied up with the twins, my two other nephews and Grayson's newborn, so Kimmie and I are hanging out."

"So many babies," she mumbled. All of them Boone's grandchildren, something she wouldn't mention again. "I've never been around children. I'm more comfortable with horses," she confessed.

"Yeah. Me, too." But then he shrugged and grinned at Kimmie when she returned the kiss to his cheek.

"Nunk," the little girl said, and she dropped her head onto his shoulder.

"That's Kimmie's version of uncle," Mason explained. He eased her back to a standing position, and Kimmie ran to the toy chest next to a leather sofa. Everything in the room was masculine except for that toy chest that was stuffed to the brim.

Mason took his gaze off his niece and turned it back on Abbie. No glare this morning. His face could never be considered soft, but she thought she could see sympathy or something in his eyes. Well, she thought that until his gaze slid over her again.

Abbie checked to make sure the concho was hidden. It was. She nearly asked if something else was wrong, but then she saw it. Not anger or even disapproval. He was looking at her the way a man looked at a woman.

Oh. *That.*

The look didn't last long, and he shifted his attention to the laptop.

"Did anyone have time to check on the horses to make

sure they're okay?" she asked. It sickened her to think
that the gunman who'd attacked them would go after the
helpless animals.

"All of them are fine." He paused. "I'll move the ones
you were training back to the pasture until I can hire someone else."

That sickened her a little, too, but there was nothing she
could do about it. After what had happened, she couldn't
stay.

Because her hands suddenly felt shaky, Abbie crammed
them in her back pockets. "You'll be driving me into
town?"

He got another look. Not one grounded in attraction
this time. His forehead bunched up.

Mason tipped his head to the breakfast tray. "Why don't
you pour yourself a cup of coffee while we talk."

Uh-oh. This couldn't be good, and Abbie doubted that
coffee would help. Although it did smell good, and her
head was throbbing from lack of both sleep and caffeine.

She went closer, poured herself a cup. "What happened?"

He motioned for her to sit in the chair next to his desk,
but she shook her head. Sipped her coffee. And waited.

"The man who set the fire and shot at us is Ace Chapman," Mason let her know. "He's a hired gun and not small
potatoes either. The FBI has had tabs on him for years and
hasn't been able to nail him, but they estimate that he's
killed more than a dozen people."

Abbie had tried to brace herself for this, but she hadn't
expected it to be this bad. Not just an assassin but one
with a deadly résumé. "How did this monster know I was
here at the ranch?"

Mason shook his head. "I haven't figured that out yet.
The P.I. agency I use for background checks is making sure

nothing was leaked. But there's a possibility that someone at the agency made your photo available to the wrong person."

"How?" she wanted to know. Her heart was starting to race now, and the coffee wasn't going down easily. Her stomach was churning.

He paused a moment. "When I interviewed you for the job, the security cameras were on. I copied an image from it and sent it to the P.I. agency along with the background request."

Oh, mercy. "You always do that?"

"Always." And he didn't sound exactly apologetic either. "I don't like to take risks with the ranch, and you'd be surprised how many lowlifes apply for jobs."

No, she wouldn't. She didn't consider Boone and herself lowlifes, but they'd often given false names and information when asking for work.

Not for this job, though.

Because she'd figured Mason would do some checking, she had given her legal name, Abbie Baker, so she could use her own social security number and provide Mason with some references. Of course, she'd only given him references that weren't likely to get back to Boone. One of them had been Marshal McKinney's own stepfather, and the other, the marshal's brother. Abbie had listed them on the job application because she'd known they wouldn't leak anything to Ferguson, and besides, she'd done good work for both.

"What did the P.I. do with my picture?" she wanted to know.

"That's what I'm checking, but as a minimum he or she would have run it past law enforcement so they could check for any priors under a different name."

Great. Ferguson no doubt still had contacts with the

cops. In fact, as badly as he wanted to find her, he'd probably paid off someone to look for any information that would lead him to her.

And it had obviously worked.

Mason checked his watch. "Vernon Ferguson should be arriving at the sheriff's office soon. Grayson wants to question him."

"So do I," Abbie jumped to say.

He shook his head. "Not a good idea."

"Ferguson already knows I'm here," she pointed out. "And he might slip and say something."

Mason gave her a flat look to remind her that wasn't likely to happen. "I can arrange for you to watch the interview. You can even give Grayson some questions to ask, but I don't want you in the same room with him. If we get lucky and are able to make an arrest, Ferguson's lawyers could toss out anything he says because of the impropriety of having you in the interrogation room."

Abbie considered that, nodded and thought back through what Mason had just told her. "Are there any solid connections between this Ace Chapman and Ferguson?"

"No." He paused, checked on Kimmie and then looked at Abbie again. "But something's not adding up."

Abbie wasn't sure where this was leading, and she didn't get a chance to ask. That's because a tall, silver-haired woman came rushing into the room.

"I can take Kimmie now so you can drive into town," she said to Mason before her attention landed on Abbie. She made a slight hmmmp sound. "This is the girl Boone's been raising?"

Mason nodded. "Abbie, this is Bessie Watkins. She takes care of the place."

"And I take care of all the Rylands, too," Bessie provided. She scooped up Kimmie but kept her weathered gaze plastered to Abbie. "So how is Boone these days?"

"He's been better," Abbie settled for saying.

It looked as if Bessie wanted to say more, maybe she even wanted Abbie to send Boone a scathing message for her, but the woman simply shrugged and patted Abbie's arm. It was the closest thing she'd gotten to a friendly welcome since the Rylands had learned of her association with Boone.

"We need to leave now, but you can bring your coffee with you," Mason said and started for the door.

That was Abbie's cue to follow him, but first she deposited the coffee cup back on his desk. Despite her need for caffeine, she couldn't finish it, not with her stomach churning over the thought of Ace Chapman and Ferguson.

Mason said goodbye to Bessie and Kimmie before he walked out and down the stairs. Abbie was right behind him, waiting for him to spill whatever he'd been about to say before Bessie came into the room.

He grabbed a black Stetson from the hooks on the wall near the door and led her outside to the truck parked at the side of the house. Not a flashy late-model vehicle. It was at least twenty years old, and the once-red paint was now scabbed with rust spots. She'd heard the ranch hands making fun of Mason's ride, and she had to wonder why a man worth millions hadn't bought something better.

She climbed inside and was surprised that the interior was spotless.

"It belonged to my granddaddy," Mason said as if he knew exactly what she was thinking. And with that meager explanation, he drove away from the ranch.

His grandfather, the one who was murdered by the senator. Abbie was certain there was more to the story than she'd heard, and she wondered if it was connected to Boone.

Or to her.

"You said something didn't add up about Ace Chapman," she reminded him.

He nodded, paused. "Chapman isn't the sort of killer who'd try to burn his victim. He's a shooter. I watched the feed from the security cameras, and he broke into the cottage before he set the fire."

Oh, God. Abbie pressed her hand to her chest to try and steady her heart. "He was inside when I was sleeping?"

"Yeah." And that's all Mason said for several moments. "He could have just killed you then. Shot you in bed. You would have never known what hit you."

That chilled her to the bone, and her breath stalled in her throat. All Abbie could do was watch the Texas landscape fly by, and of course, at that moment when she was breathless and scared beyond belief, they passed a cemetery. A reminder of death that she didn't need.

"On the security feed, I saw that Ace was holding something, and I had my brother Gage analyze it," Mason continued. "Ace was filming you as you ran from the burning cottage."

That took away the rest of her breath. Abbie turned and stared at him. "Why would he do that?"

Mason mumbled something, shook his head. "At first, before I knew he had a camera, I thought maybe he burned the cottage because there was something in it that he wanted destroyed. Something other than you. Was there?"

Abbie wasn't so quick to answer *no*. She tried to think. "Just my personal items. Clothes. My cell phone."

"Anything from or related to Boone?" he pressed.

The thoughts were jumping through her head. But so was the fear. "I had a photo of Boone and me in my wallet."

Abbie couldn't think of anything else. "Maybe this assassin just wanted to make sure there was nothing inside that could be used to link him to Boone or Vernon Ferguson."

"Maybe." But Mason didn't sound convinced. "There's another reason he could have filmed it." His pause was longer this time. Definitely a hesitation. "Maybe Ace was supposed to send the film to someone."

Abbie didn't have to think about this part. "To prove to the person who hired him that I was really dead."

Mason lifted his shoulder. "But if he'd only needed to prove you were dead, he could have set up the camera in your bedroom and shot you."

There was a chill again, and Abbie hated that her hands were trembling more with each passing moment. "What are you getting at?"

He glanced at her. "Maybe Ace was supposed to make you suffer. A fire would do that. And he would have proof of that suffering. Proof that he'd done the job someone paid him to do."

She was shaking her head before he finished, but then the head shaking came to a screeching halt. "You think Ace maybe filmed it so he could show it to someone? To torment them?" And there was only person who fit that particular bill. "Boone."

Mason made a sound of agreement, but it was somewhat lukewarm. "But why would Ferguson hire Ace to kill you and show it to Boone?"

"He wouldn't," Abbie mumbled. "If anything, Ferguson would do it the other way around. He would kill Boone to get to me. I'm the one he wants." And that caused her heart to start pounding.

This wasn't making any sense.

Unless...

She thought back to the past few weeks. Boone had

been so strange. Frightened, even. Did that have anything to do with Ace and Ferguson? Maybe. But even so, she was still the primary target. One or both was willing to kill her and then use her death in some way. Perhaps to get back at Boone.

But for what?

Was this the reason Boone had said the past was catching up with him?

Abbie's gaze flew to Mason. "I have to warn Boone about what's going on."

"I called Marshal Harlan McKinney this morning," Mason explained. "He's aware of the possible danger and will contact Boone. In fact, he's probably doing that right now."

The relief was instantaneous. And short-lived. Yes, Marshal McKinney knew how to get in touch with Boone, but would it be in time? And would it be enough?

"For now, just focus on you," Mason instructed. "Let's get past the interview with Ferguson, find Ace and then you can get back to Boone."

She nodded, knew that he was right, but Abbie couldn't stop the blasted tears from burning in her eyes. Nor could she stop the hoarse sob that escaped her throat. It was bad enough that she was in danger, but now she had Boone and the entire Ryland clan in an assassin's path.

"I need to make some kind of deal with Ferguson," she said, thinking out loud. "I have to do something to stop him."

Mason cursed and dragged her across the seat toward him. Abbie landed right against him.

"Use my shoulder," he insisted. "Go ahead and have yourself a good cry before we get to the sheriff's office. But any talk about making deals with Ferguson stops. I read the man's file, and you'd be safer dealing with the devil himself."

She wanted to say that the danger would stop if she were dead, but that might not be true. Abbie no longer had any idea what would keep everyone safe. And that tore through her heart. The tears came, despite her squeezing her eyes shut, and she wiped them away as fast as she could.

"Don't say you're sorry again," Mason grumbled when she looked up at him. "Got that?"

Because that was exactly what she was about to do, Abbie stayed quiet. She stayed put, too, even though she knew this close contact was wrong. It didn't make sense. In the middle of all of this, she shouldn't be feeling all tingly because of Mason. He hated her. And the only thing that could result from this was more trouble added to the heap of it she already had.

Abbie eased away from him.

"Those weren't many tears," he pointed out. "Or maybe it's the shoulder you object to?"

"The shoulder," she readily confirmed. She risked glancing at him. "Thanks for the offer, but leaning on your shoulder comes with a high price."

He didn't deny it. Mason just kept driving, his attention on the road ahead as they entered Silver Creek. "Yeah." And that was all he said. "I guess it's true. Opposites do attract. But in our case, it can't."

Abbie couldn't agree more. They had too much bad stuff in the way to even think about something as mundane as a kiss.

But still she thought about it.

Felt it, too. In fact, just thinking about Mason's kiss rid her of the rest of that chill. And that's the reason she moved all the way back to her side of the seat. The timing was perfect because Mason turned into the parking lot of the sheriff's office and came to a stop.

Considering the awkwardness simmering between them, Abbie would have jumped from the truck, but Mason held her back and looked around. Not an ordinary look, but a cop doing surveillance of an area where an assassin might be hiding. Abbie cursed herself for not thinking of that on her own. She'd kept herself safe for twenty-one years, and it was as if she had forgotten everything Boone had ever taught her.

"Let's go," Mason insisted when he had finished checking out the area.

He led her through the back entrance and into a hall, and they'd barely managed to make it inside when a man stepped out from one of the open doors. Judging from his appearance, this was another of Boone's sons. Also judging from the shiny badge clipped to his belt, he was a deputy sheriff.

The man's attention landed on her, and she got a scowl. Yep, definitely a Ryland.

"Abbie, this is my brother Dade," Mason said.

Dade didn't respond. He turned his attention to Mason. "Vernon Ferguson is already here. I put him in the interview room."

"Did he bring lawyers with him?" Mason asked.

"Two." Dade gave a dry smile.

Abbie was surprised Ferguson hadn't brought more. He could certainly afford it. Because he'd resigned as a police officer twenty-one years ago, he'd managed his late father's estate and apparently added even more millions to it. She doubted all those earnings had been legal.

"Grayson and Gage will start the interview in a few minutes," Dade continued. "They were just waiting for you to get here."

"Then let's get this show on the road." Mason tipped his head toward a room just up the hall, and Abbie followed him.

So did Dade but not before aiming another scowl at her.

"Did Boone ever tell you why he hated us so much that he had to leave?" Dade tossed out there.

Like the scowl, she'd expected the question or one similar to it. "No. And he never told me why he hated himself either."

Dade flexed his eyebrows and made a slight sound of amusement. "Grayson said you were the shy-and-quiet type."

Abbie mimicked the sound of disapproval Dade had made. "He was wrong." And she left it at that.

She was shy and quiet, but not when it came to defending Boone. Apparently, she would get a lot of practice doing that as long as she was around his sons. Hopefully not much longer. The first step to making that happen was this interview.

The moment she stepped into the room with Mason, she spotted Ferguson on the other side of what appeared to be a two-way mirror. Even though she knew he couldn't see her, Abbie had to force herself not to take a step back, but it was a challenge. He sat there at the iron-gray metal table in his expensive dark blue suit, flanked on each side by lawyers in equally pricey clothes.

"How long has it been since you've seen him?" Mason asked.

Unfortunately, Abbie didn't even have to think about her answer. "Five years, three months." She paused, gathered her breath. "Boone and I were working a ranch down in Laredo, and he showed up."

"Did he try to kill you?"

"I wish." But she waved that off. "It's just, if he had,

we could have had him arrested. But no. He was there to remind me that he could get to me anytime he wants. And he can. From time to time he sends me flowers. Notes. Anything to let me know I'm not safe and never will be."

Mason made another of those sounds that could have meant nothing or anything, and she watched as Grayson and his brother Gage entered the room.

"Ferguson is going through a lot of trouble to keep tabs on you," Mason commented. "Especially considering his fight was with your mother."

Abbie nodded. "He probably thinks she told me some things about him. She didn't. And if she had, I would have already gone to the cops with it."

Mason stayed quiet a moment. "Because he's obviously a warped man, maybe Ferguson wants to get back at Boone for helping you."

That made the chill in her blood even worse. Because it was exactly something that Ferguson would do. The chill quickly turned to anger, and she hated Ferguson for going after the man who'd literally saved her life.

At that exact moment, Ferguson's gaze lifted toward the mirror, and it seemed as if he knew she was there. Watching him. He smiled that oily smile she saw in her nightmares. Before she could stop herself, Abbie stepped back and tried to level her breathing.

"Marshal McKinney will offer Boone protection," Mason explained. His voice and body language didn't change, but he'd no doubt noticed her little defensive maneuver. "And he's already arranging a new identity for you. Probably not in Texas this time."

No. Not in Texas. Which meant she'd have to leave her home and her career because Ferguson would trace her that way. She might have to leave Boone, too. That might be her only chance to keep him safe if Ferguson truly had him in his sights.

And that broke her heart.

Mason adjusted the audio so they could hear Grayson explaining the reason for the interview. However, he didn't even finish before Dade appeared in the doorway of the observation room.

"We found Ace Chapman," Dade said to Mason. He had his phone sandwiched between his shoulder and his ear.

Abbie pulled in her breath. She hadn't forgotten about the hit man, of course, but Ferguson had distracted and unnerved her.

"Where?" Mason asked.

Dade lifted his index finger in a wait-a-second gesture and repeated the question to the person on the other end of the line.

A moment later, Dade cursed and drew his gun. "Ace Chapman is less than a block from here and headed this way."

Chapter Seven

Mason forced Abbie to sit down in the sole chair in the observation room. Not that it would help, but the way she was trembling, he didn't want her to fall on her face. And the chair was better than pulling her back into his arms. He wanted his arms and hands free in case Ace decided to do something stupid and storm the sheriff's office.

"Mel and I will go after Ace," Dade insisted. "You stay here with Abbie."

Mel was Deputy Melissa Garza, and between Dade and her, they had enough firepower and experience to bring down the assassin. Mason would have preferred to be in on the fight himself, especially because this was the bastard who'd fired at Abbie and him, but he couldn't take the risk. Instead, he shut the door the second Dade left. And he pulled his gun.

Pulling his gun didn't help Abbie's breathing and neither did the text he sent to Grayson to let him know what was going on. Abbie was able to see his brother's reaction and Gage's, too, when Grayson whispered the news to him.

"We have to reschedule this," Grayson informed Ferguson and his lawyers. That sent a flurry of questions and complaints from the lawyers, but Ferguson himself just smugly sat there as if he'd accomplished the chaos that he'd wanted.

"Is there a problem?" Ferguson asked Grayson when Gage got up and left. No doubt going to assist Dade and Mel.

"You tell me," Grayson fired back. "Is there?"

Ferguson lifted his shoulder in a casual shrug. "No problem that I'm aware of. I'm just doing my civic duty by voluntarily coming here to answer questions. Questions that you implied were urgent." Another shoulder lift. "Apparently, they're not so urgent after all if they can be rescheduled."

Mason wished he could muck out the stables with that arrogant face. But beside him, Abbie was having a different reaction.

"Ferguson knows what this is doing to me," she mumbled.

No doubt. Well, it was no doubt *if* Ferguson had been the one to hire Ace. Mason wasn't completely convinced that he had, and he hoped Marshal McKinney could get some answers from Boone. And getting answers from Boone was something Mason thought he'd never hear himself want.

On the other side of the glass, Ferguson checked his watch. "Well, I'm disappointed with the change in plans. I'd hoped to see Maddie this morning." He made a show of looking embarrassed, because Mason doubted it was genuine. "Oops, make that Abbie. That's what she's calling herself these days. She is here, isn't she?"

Grayson didn't answer that. "Why did you want to see her?"

Ferguson huffed as if the answer were obvious. "To give her my sympathies, of course. I heard about the fire and the shooting at your family's ranch where she's working. It's all over town. Gossips," he added in mock disgust. "I just wanted to assure her that I would do everything in my power to make certain she's safe."

That put a knot in Mason's stomach. What kind of sick game was this nutjob playing?

"You want to keep her safe?" Grayson added a flat look to go along with the question.

"I do." More mock disgust, but Mason could see the edges of a smile. "She was just a child when her mother was killed. That wasn't my fault, but you cops and the press blamed me for it." He shrugged, scraped one thumbnail with another. "Still, I can't blame Abbie for the mistakes of law enforcement."

"So you don't want her dead?" Grayson asked.

"No," Ferguson jumped to answer. "All a misunderstanding on her part. I want Abbie to be safe and happy." He turned his gaze back to the mirror. To Abbie. "I want her to be able to order white daisies for her mother's grave without having to look over her shoulder."

Abbie gasped and got to her feet. She would have started for the door if Mason hadn't latched on to her.

"He saw me. He watched me." The words rushed out with her breath. "Yesterday morning I came into town to get supplies with one of the ranch hands. I stopped by the florist to order flowers for my mother's grave. White daisies. Today would have been her birthday."

Hell. Mason made a mental note to call the P.I. agency again and see if someone there had leaked Abbie's location.

"Ferguson was stupid to admit that he knew you were in town. That means he had both motive and opportunity to send Ace after you." Even though that would be hard to prove, and Abbie's rattled sigh let him know that she was on the same page.

"I do have other appointments in town," Ferguson said after another check of his watch. "I suppose if your urgent questions haven't been answered by someone else, I could return in an hour or two."

His lawyers objected again, saying that he'd gone above and beyond to cooperate with the Silver Creek sheriff's office. They made it sound like something lower than hoof grit.

Ferguson stood, aimed another smile at Abbie. Mason put his hand on her shoulder to steady her and kept watching.

"I'm meeting with Rodney Stone and Nicole Manning at the Saddle and Spur Café," Ferguson said. "It's just up the street from here, right, Sheriff?"

Abbie could no doubt tell from Grayson's reaction that the question was a shocker. "Who are those people?" she asked Mason.

"They're connected to the late Senator Ford Herrington. Stone was his personal attorney and friend. Nicole, his longtime lover and campaign manager."

She shook her head. "Why would Ferguson be meeting with them, and why mention it to Grayson?"

"I'm not sure." Mason moved closer to the mirror and waited for Grayson to ask the question that Mason was also wondering.

Grayson didn't make him wait several seconds. "How do you know Rodney Stone and Nicole Manning?"

"You don't have to answer that," one of his lawyers advised.

But Mason could see the return of the smugness on Ferguson's slimy face. "No reason not to tell the sheriff that I contributed rather large sums of money to Senator Harrington's reelection campaigns. Ford introduced me to both of them, and we've seen each other at social engagements from time to time."

Mason didn't know why that surprised him. Both men

were rotten to the core, so, in a warped way, it seemed logical that they would have an association of some kind. Maybe they were even friends.

"Why are you meeting with the senator's former business associates?" Grayson pressed.

Ferguson smiled again. "Nicole has a book deal, one of those pillow talk, tell-all biographies, and Stone is representing her. I just want to make sure that my association with the senator will be portrayed in a good light."

Something was up, and considering this was Ferguson, it was something bad.

Ferguson snapped his fingers in an aha gesture. "You know, you Rylands should meet with Stone and Nicole, too. I mean, just to make sure she has the correct details."

"Details for what?" Grayson asked.

It was a good question considering that Mason and all his lawmen brothers were involved in the shootout that had ended with Ford's suicide. Also, considering that Nicole was dirty like her late boss and lover, there was no telling what she might say.

Ferguson smiled again. "About the affair Ford's wife had."

Oh, man. Nicole was bringing Granddaddy Chet into this? But Mason didn't have time for the anger to settle in.

"My grandfather's been dead for over twenty years," Grayson remarked. He seemed cool enough on the surface, but Mason knew he was riled underneath that lawman's exterior. "And Ford confessed to his murder. That's old news. Nothing for Nicole to rehash."

Ferguson made a sound of exaggerated surprise. "Oh, I can see you're not in the information loop. You should probably ask Nicole about this."

Grayson stood and met Ferguson eye to eye. "I'm asking *you.*"

If Ferguson was the least bit intimidated by Grayson's stance or tone, he didn't show it. "It's not my secret to tell, but I'm sure Nicole will share all the bits and pieces with you." He reached across the table and extended his hand for Grayson to shake.

Grayson ignored him and strolled out ahead of Ferguson and his lawyers. His brother entered the observation room and he shut the door.

"What's the word on Ace Chapman?" Grayson said immediately.

"Nothing yet. Mel, Gage and Dade are out there." Mason watched as Ferguson left with his attorneys in tow. "What was all that about Nicole Manning and Rodney Stone?"

Grayson shook his head and looked at Abbie. "I was hoping you could tell me."

"No," Abbie quickly answered. "Mason told me about your grandfather's murder. And about the affair he had with the senator's wife. But I don't know how or if it relates to anything else."

Grayson gave him a look, and Mason groaned. Someone would have to go digging back through that old baggage. All of the painful memories, including those of Boone. And that *someone* was Mason.

There was a sharp knock at the door, and Mason automatically moved Abbie behind him. Just in case Ferguson was making a surprise visit. But it was Dade, and he shook his head the moment he opened the door.

"Ace Chapman got away," Dade said, causing the rest of them to groan. "Mel and Gage are still out there, and we've asked the Rangers to set up a roadblock. We might get lucky."

"Might," Abbie repeated, and Mason knew what she was thinking. As long as Ace was out there, she was in

grave danger. He'd already tried to kill her twice with the fire and the shots, and he wouldn't hesitate to try again.

Grayson moved closer to her and made eye contact. "It's your choice, but it'd be smart for you to stay here awhile, in our protective custody."

It was an offer he would make to anyone in danger. It was no different with Abbie, but Mason knew this wouldn't be easy for any of them.

"Come on," Mason insisted, and he tightened the grip he had on her arm. She was looking wobbly again. "We'll go to my office. I need to make some calls."

And calm Abbie down.

Grayson and Dade went in one direction, and Mason and Abbie headed up the hall. He got her inside as fast as he could but didn't shut the door, because he wanted to hear if anyone came into the building. Especially Ace. He doubted the hit man would make a stand in the sheriff's office, but he wasn't taking any chances.

"Ferguson's been watching me," she repeated. "Why didn't he just kill me when he saw me at the florist?"

Mason tried to make her sit, but she started to pace.

"My guess? Ferguson's not the sort to do the dirty work himself. He probably found you and then called Ace. And maybe he doesn't really want you dead. In his own sick way he might want you alive so he can torture you."

She gave a shaky nod and scrubbed her hands down her arms. "But how did he find me?"

Yes, that was the big question, and because Mason still didn't have an answer, he took out his phone and scrolled through the numbers until he got to Sentron, the P.I. agency in San Antonio. He put the call on Speaker, hoping that whatever he heard wouldn't make matters worse for Abbie, and when the receptionist answered, Mason asked to speak to the owner, Burke Dennison.

"Tell me what you've learned about the background check on Abbie Baker," Mason demanded.

"Well, it's not good," Burke said, making Mason groan.

Yeah. This would make matters worse for Abbie, but Mason was positive she wasn't going to let him take the call off Speaker. Besides, she had a right to know, and he'd deal with the fallout later.

"The agent who handled the background check is Shelley Martin," Burke explained, "and when she didn't get any of the usual info in her initial run, Shelley sent out the picture to San Antonio P.D. and to other P.I. agencies around town."

Mason would have groaned louder if it would help.

"Shelley figured this Abbie Baker was hiding something, and she was just doing her job," Burke added.

Oh, she was hiding something all right. Hiding from a killer.

"One of the other P.I.s thought Abbie looked familiar so he did some digging, made some calls and figured out that she's really Madelyn Turner."

And all that digging could and would have alerted Ferguson.

"I take it this created some problems?" Burke asked.

"You bet it did. We'll talk later." Mason would blast Burke in a private conversation, but doing that now would only add to Abbie's anxiety. For now, he hung up.

Abbie pushed her hair from her face and leaned against the wall. "Too bad I'm not at the ranch so I could go for a ride. It might work off some of this jitteriness."

Mason understood. It's how he burned off dangerous energy. And he was feeling a lot of that now, especially because he was partly responsible for Ferguson finding Abbie.

He slipped his phone back in his pocket and walked

closer. What he didn't do was close the door, even though she might like some privacy when she fell apart. There was that dangerous energy in the mix now, and privacy would only fuel things that shouldn't be fueled.

Still, he went closer and stopped right in front of her. "I'm sorry," he told her. And he wondered if she realized just how rare it was for him to apologize.

Apparently she did, because Abbie managed a weary smile before her breath broke, and a sob made its way from her throat. "I only made things worse by coming to Silver Creek."

He couldn't argue with that, but most of this wasn't her fault. Of course, all of this had started with her lie about who she really was, but considering how quickly Ferguson had found her, it was a warranted lie.

Well, for the most part.

And it was that *most part* and the sob that had Mason moving even closer. He slid his arm around her waist. The warning in his head came almost immediately. *Danger ahead.* But the rest of him pretty much ignored that, and he stayed put.

Abbie looked up at him, her eyes shiny with fresh tears. "It's harder when you're nice to me," she whispered.

Mason smiled before he could stop himself. Then frowned. Then scowled, but the scowl wasn't for Abbie. It was for him. What the heck was he doing?

Apparently, he was making a mistake.

That's because he leaned in, lowered his head and brushed a kiss on her cheek. In the back of his mind, he rationalized that this was the kind of comfort they both needed. But that was a lie. Kissing her, even a cheek kiss wasn't for comfort. It was to appease this blasted attraction.

Abbie made a sound. Not a sob. But a soft murmur that sounded like a pleasure reaction. Mason tested that theory with another brush kiss. This time, though, his mouth moved to hers.

Oh, yeah.

It was pleasure all right. And bad. Very bad. That's because he didn't move, and he didn't stop with just a simple touch. He pressed harder. Moved closer. Touching her body with his. And taking the kiss of comfort to a whole new level.

Man, she tasted good.

Like something he'd searched for his entire life. And he couldn't feel that way, especially not about Abbie.

Did that stop him?

No.

Nor did the fact that his office door was wide-open, and one of his brothers could come walking in at any moment.

But Abbie thankfully had some sense left. She pulled back, met his gaze. "We should rethink this," she whispered. And then she did something that caused his body to clench, and beg. She ran her tongue over her bottom lip and made that sound of pleasure again.

He was toast.

Mason was ready to go back for a second kiss, but the jangling sound stopped him cold. Even through the hot haze in his head, he knew the sound meant that someone had just come through the front door of the sheriff's office.

He hoped like heck that it wasn't Ace Chapman.

Abbie no doubt thought the same thing because the fear, and some embarrassment, flashed through her eyes.

"Stay put," Mason warned her, and with his gun ready, he stepped into the hall, bracing himself for a showdown with a hit man.

But it wasn't Ace Chapman who had just stepped in.

Mason saw the man, and his stomach went to his knees.

Boone Ryland was back.

Chapter Eight

Abbie held her breath, waiting. But Mason didn't shoot at the person who had captured his attention. In fact, no one shot, but the building suddenly went silent.

She inched closer to Mason, looked around him, and she cursed when she spotted Boone. What the heck was he doing here?

"You asked him to come?" Mason wanted to know. Except it wasn't a question. It was a demand. And what was left of the heat from the kiss turned ice-cold. In fact, it felt as if the temperature in the entire place had dropped.

"No, I didn't ask him to come here." In fact, this was the last place Abbie wanted to see Boone, and his sons no doubt felt the same. Of course, she had a different reason. She loved him, and Silver Creek was not a safe place right now.

Abbie maneuvered around Mason. Then Dade. And finally around Grayson before she made it to the front where the petite brunette dispatcher sat with her mouth wide-open. Abbie had braced herself for a confrontation with Ace, but in some ways this might be worse.

The three brothers came forward, a united force, standing in the hall behind her.

"You shouldn't have come back," Dade tossed out to

Boone. But she figured any of them could have voiced that particular sentiment.

Boone didn't look hurt by the remark. Just resigned. But he did take a moment to study each of his sons. Because Abbie knew him so well, she saw the pride. The pain. And the swirl of emotions that Boone had tried to bury for the past two decades.

"Are you okay?" Boone asked, his attention returning to her.

"I'm fine," she lied. Even though she knew it would upset the others, she went around the reception desk and gave him a hug. Yes, it would cause more friction, if that was possible, but she needed that hug. Apparently, Boone did, too.

"Funny that you're concerned about her safety." Dade, again.

"Not funny," Boone assured him. "I'm concerned about your safety, too. About all of you."

Judging from the sound Dade made, he didn't believe him.

"Why are you here?" she whispered to Boone.

"Why are you here?" Boone repeated. "You said you were going to Austin. You lied to me."

She nodded. "I'm sorry. Believe it or not, I was trying to help."

"You should have talked to me first." He cocked his eyebrow in a gesture that reminded her of Grayson. "I heard about the fire and the shooting."

"We're investigating it," Grayson explained. "And we don't need or want your help."

She glanced back at Mason to see if he would add anything, but he just stood there glaring.

"Have you found the man Vernon Ferguson hired to kill Abbie?" Boone asked. He volleyed glances at all three of his sons.

It was Grayson who stepped forward to answer. "We're still looking for him." He paused. "You have proof that Ferguson is the one who hired the gunman?"

Boone shook his head. "No, but he's come after her before. And he had her mother gunned down right in front of her."

Even though that'd happened ages ago, it still required Abbie to take a deep breath. "Ferguson was in here earlier," she told Boone. "And he insinuated that this might be connected to Senator Herrington's suicide and the affair his wife had with your late father-in-law."

"You remember that?" Dade spoke up. "Of course you do. You ran out on us shortly thereafter. Bad timing." Dade jabbed his index finger in Boone's direction. "And if you think for one minute that we'll forgive you for that, for losing our mother, then think again."

Boone shook his head, and a weary breath left his mouth. "No. I know you won't forgive me. I didn't come for that. I came to get Abbie out of here before Ferguson tries to kill her again." He tipped his head toward the door. "We need to go."

"Not a smart move." Mason's voice sliced through the thick silence that followed Boone's request. "The hit man, Ace Chapman, is still out there."

"Men like him are always out there," Boone answered. "I've kept her safe for over twenty years."

"Have you?" Mason challenged. He walked past his brothers. "Because just last night someone tried to kill her. Twice."

Boone flinched, just a little, probably not enough for his sons to notice. But Abbie noticed.

"She shouldn't have come to Silver Creek," Boone said. A father's warning. Abbie had heard it often enough when she was a kid.

"I was worried about you," she explained.

Boone stared at her. "Well, now we're even because I'm worried about you. It's time to leave."

"She can't leave." Mason didn't raise his voice, didn't change his tone, but it got everyone's attention. "Abbie's at the center of an attempted murder and an arson investigation. She's not just the victim, she's also a witness, and I haven't even taken her statement yet."

"Then take it," Boone said on a huff. "I need to put some distance between her and Ferguson."

Mason came closer, put his hands on his hips. He also continued to scowl at his father. "Once she gives her statement, she'll need to be in protective custody. Not with you. But with me."

"You hardly know her," Boone fired back. "I can protect her as well as you can."

Because this could turn into a full-scale argument, Abbie huffed and held up her hands. "I'm standing right here and don't appreciate not being part of this discussion."

"It's not a discussion," Mason let her know. "It's an investigation, and it's not up to your foster father to determine how best to keep you safe."

Abbie wanted that, to be safe, but she didn't want to pit Mason against Boone. She turned to Boone, trying to figure out a way to calm some of his fears, but Mason's profanity stopped her cold.

"Not this," Mason grumbled. "Not now."

She followed his gaze to the front glass and spotted the couple making a beeline for the sheriff's office. The woman was tall, curvy and had perfectly styled honey-blond hair. The fifty-something man was wearing a business suit and carrying a briefcase.

Mason moved quickly. He came to the front of the reception desk, latched on to Abbie and yanked her behind him. Dade and Grayson came forward, too, and they created a human shield in front of her.

"What's wrong?" Abbie managed to ask.

"That's Rodney Stone and Nicole Manning," Mason said just as the couple stepped inside.

Abbie knew the names, of course. Ferguson had mentioned them earlier, and they were former associates of the late Senator Ford Herrington.

Nicole looked at the protective stance of the three lawmen, smiled, and her smile widened when her attention landed on Boone.

"The patriarch returns home," Nicole said, her voice an annoying purr.

"Just visiting," Boone insisted. "What brings you here?"

"Just visiting," Stone repeated. His voice wasn't a purr, more like a growl, and he wasn't smiling either.

"You know them?" Abbie whispered to Boone.

He nodded.

"Boone and I go way back," Nicole provided. She paused and dropped the smile when she turned to Grayson. She glanced behind him at Abbie. "So this is the woman you're trying to protect?"

"Not trying," Mason snapped. "We *are* protecting her."

"Good luck with that," Nicole mumbled. "We're here to see Vernon Ferguson."

Grayson lifted his shoulder. "He's gone, said he was meeting you two at the Saddle and Spur."

"He didn't show," Stone barked. "He's late, and I'm tired of waiting for him."

"That sounds like a personal problem to me," Mason replied. "But because you're here, maybe you wouldn't mind answering some questions. Ferguson said you plan to reveal some *secrets* in your book."

"A few," Nicole smugly volunteered.

"She's playing with fire," Stone interrupted, and he shot her a glare. "Sometimes, secrets are best kept that way." He checked his watch. "I have to go."

"What secrets?" Abbie asked when Stone reached for the door. She stepped out from behind Mason, something he obviously didn't like because he tried to block her again.

"Oh, don't worry. They don't pertain to you. Well, not directly." Nicole aimed her sick, secretive smile at Boone.

"If you have something to say to me, just come out and say it," Boone told her.

"No, thanks." Yet another dose of smugness. "You'll have to wait for the book."

"While this conversation is riveting," Stone said with sarcasm dripping from his voice, "I'm done here. If Ferguson shows, tell him to call me." And with that order she doubted the Rylands would relay, he turned and walked out.

"You'll have to excuse him," Nicole said. "Stone's a bit of a sourpuss these days. I think there are some legal issues with Ford's will. Something's making him testy."

And Abbie couldn't help but wonder if this was connected to Ace and the fire. All of it was certainly connected to the Rylands, and Boone was especially uncomfortable.

Nicole checked her own watch. "Must run. Sorry to have bothered you." She fluttered her perfectly manicured nails at them in a goodbye gesture and walked out.

"What the hell was that all about?" Mason asked, turning his attention directly to Boone.

Abbie was about to assure Mason that Boone had nothing to do with this, but Boone's expression said otherwise.

What was going on?

However, before Abbie could ask Boone some questions of her own, the phone rang. When the dispatcher-receptionist answered it, Abbie realized they should

probably wait and have this conversation in private. She
didn't know the woman at the desk, and therefore she didn't
know if everything being said here would be blabbed all
over town.

"What's wrong, Tina?" Grayson asked the woman
who'd just answered the phone.

Abbie turned, looked at the dispatcher to see what had
prompted Grayson's question. Her face said it all. The
woman turned ashy pale.

"The caller says he's Ace Chapman," she relayed, and
she handed the phone to Grayson. "He says don't bother
trying to trace the call because he's using a prepaid cell."

Abbie's stomach knotted. Her chest became tight. And
just like that, she was taken right back to the nightmare
of nearly being killed.

Mason moved closer to Abbie, both of them with their
gazes fastened to Grayson as he put the phone to his ear.
But Grayson wasn't saying anything. He was just listening.
Several moments later, he handed the phone back to Tina.

"Was it Ace?" Mason immediately asked.

"Hard to tell, but he claims he is." He looked at Boone.
"Ace said I'm to give you a message—if you'll surrender
to him, he won't harm Abbie."

"What?" Abbie couldn't ask that fast enough. She
snapped toward Boone. "Why would he ask you to do
something like that? Do you know him?"

"No, I don't." Boone went to her and ran his hand down
the length of her arm. "But it's not a bad offer."

Abbie had to get past the gasp in her throat before she
could speak. "How can you say that?" She pushed his hand
away so she could latch on to him. "What's going on?"

Mason got right in Boone's face. "Do you know who
hired Ace?"

"I'm guessing it's Ferguson."

"A guess?" Mason challenged. He stared at his father. "Start talking. Tell us why this is happening."

"I have no way of knowing that, but I do know men like Ferguson, and he probably figures this is a way of making Abbie suffer."

"It would work," she let him know, "if you were going out there. But you aren't."

Boone gave weary sigh. "It might put an end to things with Ferguson."

"And it could get you killed!" Abbie fired back. She turned to Mason for help, figuring it was a long shot at best.

"If you know men like Ferguson, then you also know he's a liar," Mason stated. "Yeah, he might have you gunned down to hurt Abbie, but he could be doing this to get you out of the way. As you pointed out, you've kept her alive for over twenty years." Mason shrugged. "Ferguson might believe his best shot at her is to get you out of the way."

The argument was dead-on, something Abbie wished she'd thought to say. Hard to think rationally, though, when her thoughts were racing and she might be on the verge of losing the man she considered to be her father.

Boone's jaw tightened. The muscles stirred there. But he finally nodded. "So, how do we stop him?"

"There's no *we* in this." Mason met his stare with one of his own. "You leave Silver Creek, and I put Abbie in protective custody."

"Boone needs protection, too," Abbie pointed out.

That suggestion went over like a lead balloon. All but Tina scowled at her, and the woman seemed as confused and frightened as Abbie was.

Boone looked at Mason again. "Keep Abbie safe. Don't make her pay for the things I did wrong."

Mason didn't respond, other than a deepening scowl. Boone gave a nod to the others before turning to her.

Boone opened the door and glanced at her over his shoulder. "I'll be here in town when it's safe for you to leave."

She was about to nod, but without warning Mason again shoved her behind him.

"Get down!" Grayson shouted.

From the corner of her eye, Abbie saw the split second of movement next to the building across the street from the sheriff's office. It was a man, dressed all in black. And before it could even register in Abbie's mind, he fired a shot.

It slammed into the glass next to Boone's head.

Boone dived to the floor. Mason and Abbie did the same, and Mason practically crawled over her and came up ready to fire. Boone also pulled the Colt that he always carried in the back waist of his jeans.

Another shot crashed into the dispatcher's desk. Tina screamed, and there was a scurry of movement. Dade and Grayson were no doubt getting the woman out of the line of fire.

Boone aimed the Colt, pulled the trigger. Just as the shooter darted behind the building and out of sight.

"It's Ace Chapman," Mason relayed to the others.

Of course. Who else? Ferguson wasn't going to do this himself, but she wouldn't be surprised if he were close by, watching all of this.

"Stay down," Mason warned her, and he levered himself up. For a moment she thought he was only shifting position, but he moved off her. "Switch places with me," he told Boone.

"No!" Abbie managed to say. She didn't want either of them up and moving, but neither listened to her.

Another shot came crashing through the glass front

door. It was reinforced with metal wire so the glass didn't shatter, but the next shot splintered some wood on the desk.

"I'm coming up," Mason said. "Everybody else stay down."

She wanted to shout no again because whatever he had in mind had to be dangerous. Of course, being pinned down by a hit man wasn't exactly safe. Abbie reminded herself that Mason was an experienced lawman.

That didn't help.

She was just as terrified for his safety and prayed that Ace wouldn't shoot Mason or anyone else to get to her.

Mason scurried to the doorway. It happened fast but in slow motion, too. Her heart and head were pounding. Her stomach, churning. But because she wasn't armed, there was nothing she could do but lie there beside Boone and watch.

Mason was fast. He came up on one knee, and in the same motion he took aim.

He fired.

Not one shot but two, loud thick blasts that roared through the room and through her. Boone threw his arm over her, pushing her all the way to the floor so that she couldn't see what was happening.

However, she did hear Mason curse.

Oh, mercy. Something was wrong.

"Get an ambulance," Mason shouted. *"Now!"*

Chapter Nine

Mason could only stand and watch the ambulance speed away with Ace Chapman inside. The medic, Tommy Watters, had mumbled something about the man's condition "not looking good." Mason couldn't argue with that. They'd be darn lucky if the hit man pulled through this.

"You did what you had to do," Grayson reminded Mason. Again.

But it was a reminder that didn't help much. In most situations like this, Mason would have shot to kill. This time, though, he'd tried to neutralize Ace while keeping him alive.

So they would have a chance of Ace telling them who'd hired him.

That chance was slim to none right now. Ace had moved at the last second when Mason had fired, and instead of Mason's shot going into the man's shoulder, it had slammed into his chest. He'd gone down hard and fast.

"If Ace says anything, Dade will hear it," Grayson added.

Yeah, Dade might because he was riding in the ambulance and would no doubt stay at the hospital until there was some kind of update. But unless Ace regained consciousness, a confession wasn't likely.

That meant they were back to having a lot of questions and no real answers.

Mason turned and headed back into the sheriff's office to check on Abbie and the others. No one else had been shot, thank God, but one look at Abbie's face and he knew she hadn't come out of this unscathed.

She was seated in the chair across from his desk. Not alone. Boone was standing by her side with his hand stroking the back of her hair. Across the hall, Tina, the dispatcher, was having a crying meltdown in Grayson's office. His brother was on the phone rounding up the rest of the deputies to help with the investigation.

Mason stepped in the doorway of his office, and Abbie immediately got to her feet. "Did Ace say anything?" she asked with way too much hope in her voice.

He shook his head, dashing those hopes to the floor. "Dade will keep us updated." And then he slid his gaze to Boone. Mason didn't say a word, but he figured his unfriendly expression would do the trick.

It did.

"I'll be out front," Boone mumbled.

"Not outside," Abbie said. No more hope, just alarm in her tone and on her face.

"No. I'll be in reception," Boone assured her.

Mason stepped back, way back, so that Boone could get past him without getting close. He didn't even look at the man who'd fathered him. Instead, Mason kept his attention on Abbie.

"You okay?" he asked her.

She made a sound, part laughter, that had nothing to do with humor. "I should be used to this by now."

"No one should be used to this," he mumbled. Even though Texas-sized warning bells were going off in his head, Mason went to her anyway and pulled her into his arms.

The bells went silent.

Everything else in his head got louder. He knew he should back away, but he didn't.

Abbie eased back, looked up at him. "I should be used to this now, too." She glanced down at his arms wrapped around her. "You've been doing it a lot lately. Don't get me wrong," she quickly added, "I like it. In fact, I need it. But I know how much it's costing you."

Yeah, there was a price tag on it all right. Each time he was with her, his thoughts drifted to sex. Nothing permanent. He never thought past the seasons of the ranch. But even a one-night stand with Abbie meant he had to get past her relationship with Boone.

Mason shrugged.

If this heat inside him kept building, he could probably get past anything, and that wasn't good either.

"Most people are scared of me," he reminded her, hoping it would cause her to back away and put an end to this.

"I know," she mumbled. No backing away. She moved closer, resting her head against his shoulder.

Oh, mercy. Her body was warm and she practically sank into him. That warmth gave his own body some bad ideas, like taking her back to the ranch and to his bed.

"Don't worry," she whispered. "I'll be out of your life soon."

Mason made a sound of agreement, but the agreement didn't settle well in his mind. It was probably the forced camaraderie from the danger that was stirring the attraction. Not that the attraction needed anything to stir it. It was there, plain and simple, and even if his body was starting to ache for Abbie, Mason knew it wasn't wise for it to happen.

He backed away to tell her that, but his cell rang before he could get out a word. Hoping that it was an update from Dade, he looked at the screen. Not Dade. But it was someone Mason had expected to call.

"Marshal McKinney," Mason greeted. He put the call on Speaker. "Thanks for getting back to me. I have Abbie with me now."

"Good. I heard about the shooting. Was she hurt?"

"No," Mason and she answered in unison.

"Good," the marshal repeated. And added what sounded to be a breath of relief. "Abbie, I'm working on your identity reassignment now and should have everything together in a day or two. Until then, I need you to remain in Deputy Ryland's protective custody. Will there be a problem with that?"

She looked at him, and Mason could almost tell what she was thinking. Yes, it would be a problem, but the alternative was worse. Just because Ace was out of commission, it didn't mean his boss wouldn't just hire someone else.

"I can stay here," she said to the marshal, but she gave Mason a questioning stare.

He shrugged. Then nodded. Which, of course, made it seem as if he were indifferent or opposed. He wasn't. He wanted Abbie safe, especially because the photo to the P.I. had likely been the trigger that had put her in danger.

"Will Boone Ryland be relocating with you?" the marshal asked her.

"Yes." She dodged Mason's gaze. "In fact, he could be Ferguson's target now. Ace Chapman called right before he attacked, and he wanted Boone to *surrender* to him."

"Any idea why?" McKinney asked.

"No, but I'm hoping we'll find out."

"Vernon Ferguson is in town," Mason informed McKinney. "Either my brother or I will question him again, maybe put some pressure on him."

"I doubt he'll crack," the marshal said. "But it won't hurt to try."

No, it wouldn't. Well, it wouldn't as long as Mason could keep Ferguson far away from Abbie.

Mason ended the call and looked down at her. "I need to take you back to the ranch."

She didn't argue, not exactly. "I have to talk to Boone first."

Of course she did. Mason stepped aside and had her go ahead of him, but he also followed her to the front reception area where Boone was standing and looking out the broken glass door.

"You're leaving?" Boone turned and immediately asked her.

Abbie nodded. "Marshal McKinney is making arrangements for us, but in the meantime I'll be at the ranch. I just wanted to make sure you were headed someplace safe."

"I am," he promised. Boone shut the partially shattered door, hooked his arm around her and brushed a kiss on her forehead. Yet another fatherly gesture that had Mason's blood boiling.

Boone must have noticed Mason's reaction because he eased away from Abbie. Mason's temper cooled, and he reminded himself that Abbie needed a fatherly shoulder right now. Still, that didn't mean he was going to play nice when it came to Boone.

"You'll keep her safe?" Boone asked.

That pushed Mason's ornery button. Of course, anything Boone said was likely to do that. "Yeah, but not because you're asking." In case Boone had forgotten, Mason tapped the badge on his belt.

And Mason cursed himself.

Because Abbie saw the badge tap, and she looked as if he'd slugged her. Great. That kiss, the hugs and dirty thoughts were bleeding over into the job. And that could be a massive mistake.

"When things settle down," Boone said, "I'd like to visit your mother's grave."

"No." And Mason didn't hesitate. "The cemetery's too close to the ranch, and I don't want you there."

"I could use the back way and come up from the other end of the creek," Boone offered. "None of you would have to see me."

"But we'd know. Besides, it's in bad taste to visit a woman you helped put in the grave." Mason snapped toward Abbie. "Ready?" It wasn't a suggestion.

However, before she could answer or move, Boone spoke. "We need to talk. Not about the cemetery or ranch. I'll stay away like you want. But we need to talk."

Mason was about to say they had nothing to discuss, but there he was again, letting personal stuff get in the way. Truth was, they might have something to talk about.

"You're sure you don't know Ace Chapman?" Mason asked. Yeah, he'd already asked something similar, but he hadn't like the answer he'd gotten then.

Boone looked him straight in the eye. "I never met him in my life." He paused. "But there are some things I need to tell you and your brothers."

Mason held up his hand. "We're not taking a trip down memory lane here."

Boone blew out a long, weary breath. "We have to," he insisted. "I need to tell you what happened twenty years ago that caused me to leave."

"No," Mason said through clenched teeth. "None of us want to hear it."

"You need to hear it," Boone calmly said. "Because what happened then could be the reason Ace Chapman just tried to kill us."

ABBIE FROZE AND MENTALLY repeated what Boone had just said. "The attack is related to something you did?" she asked, praying the answer would be no.

But Boone didn't say no. He tipped his head to the hall. "Why don't we take this into Grayson's office?"

Her attention darted to Mason, to see how he was reacting to all of this, and he was just as shocked as she was. Except his was mixed with anger.

Mason aimed his index finger at Boone. "This better not be some trick to get us to listen to your sob story."

"It's not," Boone assured him, and he walked past them toward Grayson's office.

Mason and she followed. "You know what this is about?" Mason asked her.

"Don't have a clue." But Abbie hoped it didn't make things worse.

Boone went into Grayson's office, and Grayson looked at his brother first. "He said he's got something to say about Ace Chapman," Mason snarled.

Grayson's mouth tightened, and he ended his call and slipped his phone back in his pocket. "Then say it fast," Grayson ordered. "Because I'm busy."

Despite that hurry-up tone, Boone took his time answering. "Twenty-one years ago your granddaddy Chet started investigating Ford Herrington. Ford wasn't a senator then. He owned a couple of successful businesses in the county, and Chet thought Ford was involved in an illegal land deal to expand one of those businesses."

"Old news," Mason snarled. "I studied Ford's file, and I know all about that deal. There's no proof that Ford was personally involved. That's why neither Chet nor anybody else ever arrested him."

"The night he was killed, Chet went out to the Herrington estate to question Ford's wife, Sandra." Boone continued as if he hadn't heard Mason.

"We know that Granddaddy Chet had an affair with Sandra," Grayson interrupted. "Ford admitted that right before he killed himself."

"Ford was wrong," Boone said. That grabbed Abbie's attention and created a heavy silence in the room. "Chet wasn't having an affair with Sandra," Boone continued. "I was."

Abbie was sure she blinked. Until a month ago she hadn't even realized that Boone had known the late senator, so this was the first she was hearing about Herrington's wife.

"You had an affair?" Mason demanded. But it wasn't just a simple question. No, it was laced with suspicion and anger. Especially the anger.

Boone nodded. "It didn't last long, and it was a huge mistake. By the time Chet showed up that night, Sandra and I were already ending things."

The silence returned, and the brothers exchanged glances. "Mom knew?" Grayson asked.

"I don't think so." Boone cursed under his breath. "Chet didn't know, not until that night when he found Sandra and me together."

Abbie went closer. "What happened?"

Again, Boone took his time answering. "Chet was furious. Understandable. I was cheating on his daughter—"

"And you had six kids at home," Mason snapped.

"Yes," Boone acknowledged. Staring at Mason. "Like I said, it was a bad mistake. And it got worse." He paused. "Ford showed up at his house, too, while I still there, and he was suspicious. He said he knew that Sandra was having an affair, and rather than let Ford go to your mother and tell her, Chet lied and told Ford that he was the one who'd been seeing Sandra."

"Granddaddy Chet lied to protect you?" Mason pressed.

"And to protect your mother," Boone verified. "Ford was furious and out of control. He said he'd kill Sandra and make it look like an accident or suicide."

Mason cursed, and his brother wasn't far behind with the profanity. "You didn't bother to tell anyone this?" Grayson snarled.

"There wasn't time." Boone wearily dragged his hands over his face. "Chet told me to leave, and I did. Because I was stupid and thought he could handle things. I went to a bar, got drunk, and when I was leaving to go home two of Ford's bodyguards grabbed me and took me to a storage warehouse in San Antonio."

Abbie looked at Mason to see if he'd known any of this. Judging from his stunned expression, the answer was *no*.

"That same day Chet was gunned down in what was supposedly a botched robbery attempt," Boone went on. "And then Sandra drowned in the creek." His gaze came to Mason's again. "Neither was an accident. Ford either had them killed or he did it himself."

Mason opened his mouth, closed it. It took him several moments to speak. "You kept this to yourself?"

"I couldn't tell anyone," Boone insisted.

Mason huffed and aimed a scowl at his father. Abbie wanted to intercede; she wanted to do something to defuse the tension, but she didn't know where to start. She'd known Boone was troubled after the senator's suicide, and this might be the reason. Well, at least the beginning of the reason.

"You said Ford's bodyguards took you to a warehouse," she said to get the conversation moving again. "What did Ford do to you?"

"Everything," Boone whispered, and he repeated it. "Ford came to me and gave me an order to leave town."

"Why didn't he just kill you like he did the others?" Grayson fired back.

"Because I told him I'd recorded the conversation in which he threatened to kill Sandra and make it look like an accident. I didn't. It was a lie. A bluff," Boone corrected. "And that's when Ford threatened to kill one of you. I couldn't let that happen."

Abbie pulled in her breath. Even though this had happened over twenty years ago, she could still hear the pain, fresh and raw, in Boone's voice. However, she could also see that same pain in Grayson's and Mason's faces.

"So you worked out some kind of blood deal with Ford?" Grayson asked.

"I guess you could call it that. It benefited Ford, that's for sure. He said he'd let all of you live if I left town and the tape recording never surfaced."

Abbie's stomach dropped.

But Mason's reaction was less extreme. He gave Boone a flat look. "Again, why didn't you tell anybody this?"

"Because I didn't want any of you to die."

"Someone did die," Grayson pointed out. "Our mother committed suicide because you left."

"Your mother had battled depression most of her life." Boone mumbled something else that Abbie didn't catch. "And Ford pushed her over the edge by telling her about the affair. I didn't know that until after the fact. Ford paid me a visit and gloated about how she'd fallen apart when he told her that I'd slept with Sandra."

Oh, mercy. The color drained from Mason's face. Grayson didn't fare much better. He turned, dropped down into the chair behind his desk and buried his face in his hands.

Despite his pain, Mason faced Boone head-on. "How

did Ford find out his wife had the affair with you and not with Granddaddy Chet?"

"Sandra told him right before he killed her. That's when Ford realized he'd murdered the wrong man."

Their grandfather had died for no reason. Well, no reason other than letting Ford believe he was sleeping with Sandra Herrington.

"If you'd told someone sooner, we could have caught Ford," Mason insisted. "And you wouldn't have put the family through hell and back."

"I tried to catch him." Boone leaned against the wall and let it support him. "I tried for years, but Ford was too smart for me. He never left a trace of himself behind."

"Until he committed suicide," Abbie mumbled. She gave that some thought and shook her head. "I saw you reading the newspapers about the suicide, but you didn't seem relieved."

"I wasn't," Boone admitted.

That caused Mason to huff. "I guess because you no longer had a reason to stay gone."

"No." Boone looked away. "Because I had an even bigger reason to stay gone."

Abbie was certain she'd misheard Boone. "What do you mean?"

But Boone didn't get a chance to answer. That's because the bell over the front door jangled, and after the shooting, everyone was clearly on edge. Both Mason and Grayson drew their guns, and Boone stepped in front of her—just as Mason tried to do the same. They ended up colliding shoulders, causing Mason to shoot his father a glare.

Grayson stepped out in the hall, his attention locked on the front. And he cursed. "What are you doing here?" he asked, and it wasn't a friendly question.

"I heard you had some trouble," the visitor said.

Abbie groaned because she recognized that voice—Vernon Ferguson.

"Stay put," Mason warned her.

But he didn't and neither did Grayson and Boone. They all waltzed out of the room to deal with the man after *her.* Well, Abbie was tired of hiding out and letting them fight her battles. Tired of what this was doing to the Rylands. So despite the warning, she stepped out as well, and Ferguson snagged her gaze right away.

He gave her an oily smile. "Abbie, I'd hoped to run into to you today."

"Did you figure I'd be dead?" she fired back, earning her a first-class glare from all the Ryland males. She returned the look and elbowed her way past them to face Ferguson.

"Dead?" Ferguson made a tsk-tsk sound. "I hear an accusation coming on." He made a sweeping motion toward the bullet-riddled glass. "I suppose now you're going to ask me if I hired the person to do this?"

"You bet I am," Abbie answered.

"Abbie," Mason warned again. "You shouldn't be doing this."

"We all do a lot of things we shouldn't do." And she aimed that at Boone for keeping secrets all these years. Yes, he had a good reason for keeping things quiet—so he could protect his sons—but they wouldn't be here if it weren't for his affair with a married woman.

"I'm sure you already know the hit man's name is Ace Chapman," Abbie supplied to Ferguson. Mason caught onto her to keep her from going closer, but she threw off his grip. "So did you hire him?"

"Of course not." His light, off-the-cuff tone didn't help her suddenly surly mood.

"You're a coward, you know that? You get people to

fight your fight." Abbie didn't wait for him to respond. "My mother wasn't a coward. She stood up to you and testified against you."

Ferguson's eyes narrowed, and Mason stepped directly in front of her, cutting off her view of the reaction she'd caused in the weasel who'd tormented her for most of her life.

"And look where that got your mother," Ferguson calmly said.

Nothing could have held her back at that point. *Nothing.* Abbie came out from behind Mason and rushed around the counterlike desk that divided the entrance from the rest of the building. She made it to Ferguson with Mason right on her heels and with Boone moving in from the side, and it was Mason who stepped between them at the last second. Boone grabbed Ferguson.

"It's time for you to leave," Mason told the man while he used his brute strength to keep Abbie behind him.

Ferguson stared them both down. "Of course." There wasn't even a touch of emotion in his voice. "But I'm not the threat here." Ferguson threw off Boone's grip. "He is."

Abbie quit struggling to get past Mason, and she looked at Boone, waiting for him to deny it.

But he didn't.

Mason obviously noticed the lack of denial, too, because he stared at his father. "What's he talking about?"

"Tell them," Ferguson taunted. "Tell them that the reason Abbie was nearly killed was because of you."

Again, Boone didn't deny it, and that robbed Abbie of her breath.

"I told you the truth about that deal I cut with Ford," Boone finally said. He let that hang in the air for several seconds. "But I didn't tell you that Ford promised he would reach out from the grave to ensure I never came back to Silver Creek."

Ferguson smiled again. "What Boone is fumbling to say is that Ford left instructions to have him—and all the rest of you—murdered."

Chapter Ten

Mason hadn't thought this investigation could get any crazier, but he'd been wrong. Abbie clearly thought the same because she just stood there with a stunned look on her face. The only one who wasn't gob smacked was Ferguson, and he was enjoying this way too much.

Mason did something about that.

"You're leaving now," Mason ordered the snake who'd just delivered the latest bombshell, and he moved closer to let Ferguson know he would be tossed out if he didn't obey. Mason wanted details of this beyond-the-grave mess, and he didn't want to discuss anything else in front of the man who'd tried to kill Abbie.

Well, Ferguson was probably the one who'd hired Ace to kill her.

However, after this latest revelation, Mason had to rethink that. Boone certainly wasn't jumping to say that Ferguson's claims weren't true.

Ferguson gave them an exaggerated wave, another of those blasted smiles, and he walked out.

"Start talking," Grayson demanded the moment Ferguson was out of earshot. He had his narrowed eyes aimed at Boone, and Mason made sure his glare let Boone know that he would explain everything.

Boone nodded and gave a heavy sigh. "All those years

ago when Ford threatened to kill you and your brothers, I told him that I'd kill him first. He laughed and said it was already too late for that, if he didn't call off his goons within the next ten minutes that at least two of you would be gunned down."

That required Mason to take a deep breath. All of his brothers had been young then, especially Gage and Kade. Heck, they'd been barely eleven and twelve. Just kids. The idea of a hired gun killing them tore at him hard.

"You believed Ford?" Mason clarified.

"Oh, yeah. He'd just murdered his wife and your grand-father. I didn't think it'd be much of a stretch for him to add two of my boys to the list."

Boys. That hit hard, too. Mason had been sixteen and his father's right-hand man at the ranch. Mason had wanted to be just like him. Until Boone walked out. And then Mason had just wanted him gone and out of their lives forever.

"What about Ford leaving instructions to kill us after his death?" Mason pressed.

Boone nodded, a muscle flickering in his jaw. "The same day that Ford ran me out of town, he said I couldn't come back. *Ever.* I said I'd come back as soon as I put him in the grave."

"You threatened to kill him?" Abbie asked.

Boone met her gaze. "I would have killed him, but he showed me a letter. It was instructions that in the event of his death, me and my entire family were to be killed." He paused. "I didn't think it was a bluff."

No, not from Ford. He wasn't the bluffing type. And that meant the danger was just starting.

For all of them.

Abbie stepped closer to Mason, her arm brushing against his, and she looked up at him as if she knew ex-actly what this was doing to him. And what it was doing was tearing him apart. He didn't want to go through this again. Didn't want to relive the memories of the god-awful past. He just wanted to toss Boone out and go back a couple of days.

But then Mason glanced down at Abbie.

Going back would mean there'd been no rescue, no kiss. No gentle arm brush. And that was a good thing.

Okay, it wasn't, and all the lies he told himself wouldn't change that.

That caused Mason to mentally curse again. He wasn't sure why it was good to have Abbie here, but for the first time in a long while, he felt he had someone on his side. Even if having her there would complicate the heck out of an already-complicated situation.

"I don't know who Ford instructed to kill us," Boone continued. "I don't know who got that letter. That's what I've been trying to find out since the moment I heard Ford had committed suicide."

"Lynette," Grayson said, taking the name right out of Mason's mouth. "I'll call her." He turned and headed up the hall in the direction of his office.

Abbie looked at Mason again. "Lynette?"

"Ford's daughter. She's married to my brother Gage. She and her father weren't exactly close." That was a massive understatement. Right before his death, Ford had tried to kill both Gage and Lynette despite the fact that Lynette was pregnant. "Still, she might know something."

But Abbie shook her head. "Ford died nearly a month ago. Why didn't this assassin he'd hired come after all the Rylands then? He might not have been able to find Boone, but the rest of you were all here in Silver Creek."

Unfortunately, Mason had an explanation for that. "Ford's will was read just two days ago."

And shortly thereafter, there'd been the fire and then

Ace Chapman's attacks. Knowing what he'd just learned, it was hard for Mason to believe that it was all a coincidence.

But something still wasn't right here.

"If this was Ford's doing, then why set the fire that could have killed Abbie?" Mason asked.

All of them looked at each other for several moments, and it was Boone who finally spoke. "Maybe to make me suffer. If Ford found out that I'd practically raised Abbie, he might want her dead along with my sons."

"Or," Abbie said and then paused. "The fire and the attempts to kill me are all Ferguson's doing." Another pause. Her breath trembled a little. "Maybe Ford's assassin is just getting started."

Hell.

Mason couldn't discount that. There could be two forces working against all of them, but that meant that Abbie could be a target from both sides. Abbie must have realized that, too, because the color drained from her face.

"Come on." Mason caught onto her arm. "I'll get you a drink of water. I also need to see what I can find out about Ace Chapman's condition."

Mason took a step. Abbie didn't. "What about you?" she asked Boone.

He shrugged and dropped down into one of the reception chairs. "I'll wait around and see what Grayson learns from Lynette."

Abbie nodded. "I won't be long."

Mason didn't miss the loving tone she used nor the loving look Boone gave her in return. Like father and daughter. Ironic. Mason had always heard his mother say that Boone had wanted a daughter. Well, now he had one. And he'd lost all his sons in the process.

Abbie followed Mason down the hall, and they paused at Grayson's doorway. His brother was still on the phone with Lynette, so Mason went to his own office and took a bottle of water from the fridge.

"I thought you were going to rip Ferguson's eyes out," Mason said when he handed her the water. He also motioned for her to sit because she didn't look too steady on her feet.

"I thought I was, too." Abbie didn't sit, but she did look up at him. "You stopped me. I'm not sure I want to thank you for that."

Mason nearly smiled. *Nearly.* And then he remembered how the scumbag had made Abbie's life a living hell. "If he'd touched you, I would have had to shoot him. I don't want that. Not yet. Not until we're sure he's called off his dogs. It won't do us any good if he's dead and the attacks continue."

"So you do think Ferguson is behind the attacks?"

"Maybe." He rethought that. "But Ford was just as dirty, just as dangerous as Ferguson, and I wouldn't put it past him to try to get some revenge."

She groaned, shook her head. That's when Mason decided to push the sitting idea again. He took her by the arm and eased her into the chair. "Stay put, drink your water and I'll make some calls."

She nodded, but there was no agreement in her eyes. "I know it hurts when you see Boone with me."

Mason settled for a shrug.

"I know it hurts," Abbie repeated. She paused, drank some water. "All those years he wasn't happy. I never knew why, of course. And that's a roundabout way of saying that he never stopped loving any of you."

Mason wanted to believe that, but believing would mean letting go of the past. He wasn't ready for that. "Remember, I put a bullet through the silver concho he gave me."

GET 2 BOOKS

We'd like to send you two *Harlequin Intrigue*®
novels absolutely free. Accepting them puts you under
no obligation to purchase any more books.

HOW TO GET YOUR
2 FREE BOOKS AND 2 FREE GIFTS

1. Return the reply card today, and we'll send you two
   Harlequin Intrigue novels, absolutely free! We'll even
   pay the postage!

2. Accepting free books places you under no obligation
   to buy anything, ever. Whatever you decide, the free
   books and gifts are yours to keep, free!

3. We hope that after receiving your free books you'll
   want to remain a subscriber, but the choice is yours–
   to continue or cancel, any time at all!

EXTRA BONUS

**You'll also get two free mystery gifts!
(worth about $10)**

Abbie stood, slowly, and placed the water on the edge of his desk. "I'm sorry, too, about the affair that Boone had."

That put a damper on the cozy, protective feeling he had when looking down at Abbie. "Don't apologize for him."

"I'm not," she insisted. "I'm telling *you* that I'm sorry because it must hurt, even after all these years."

"It does." And he wanted to hit himself for that too-easy but too-true confession.

Now it was Abbie who touched his arm. Not a good time for it with the air zinging, but Mason didn't stop her. "I knew their marriage wasn't perfect." And he had to pause. "My mother was on antidepressants and would go into these dark moods where she wouldn't come out of her room for days."

"I'm sorry," Abbie repeated.

"It was a long time ago," he assured her. Mason lifted his shoulder. "Still, I didn't know Boone had slept with Sandra Herrington."

Abbie made a sound of agreement. "It apparently set a lot of bad things in motion."

Mason couldn't argue with that, but he was an adult now, and even though he didn't want to give Boone an inch, he could see the situation through adult eyes. That didn't mean he could forgive Boone, but Mason knew where the bulk of the blame belonged. On Ford Herrington.

A dead man.

"You're not scowling," he heard Abbie say, and that snapped his attention back to her.

Because a glare and a scowl were his usual expressions, he had to think about that for a second or two. He certainly hadn't been thinking good thoughts, so maybe it had something to do with that arm rub.

Mason stared at her. She stared back. And it was one of those moments where he could see pretty much what she was thinking, and whether it was good or bad, Abbie was just as puzzled about him as he was about her.

She shook her head, drew back her hand so that she was no longer touching him. "Just to let you know, I don't make it a habit of doing this."

Doing what? flickered through his mind. But a flicker was all the time he had because she came up on her toes, slid her hand around the back of his neck and kissed him.

The jolt was instant. And nice. It slid through him like the blazing Texas heat, and while part of him remembered that this just wasn't a good idea, he couldn't remember why it wasn't.

Mason hooked his arm around Abbie's waist, gathered her into his arms and kissed her right back. He figured if he was going to make things worse that at least it should aim for making them feel better first. And feeling better was exactly what happened.

Yeah, there was that blasted heat that got even hotter when her breasts pressed against his chest. But there was more than heat. The taste of her, like sweet summer wine. And the feel of her mouth beneath his. She was soft in all the right places, and one place in particular made Mason hard as stone.

She pulled back, gasping a little, and looking more than stunned. Mason knew how she felt. He was pretty sure that kiss shouldn't have felt that good, and Abbie's taste shouldn't still be on his lips.

Oh, man.

And Mason just kept mentally repeating that.

The corner of her mouth lifted. "Now you're scowling."

He met her gaze. "I don't want to want you."

"Yes." She brushed her lips over his again. "I know."

Their gazes held, and Mason had no idea what he could say to cool this down, but he figured he had to say something. He didn't get that something out, however, before he heard the footsteps. They stepped away from each other. But not in time. His brother Dade appeared in the doorway and gave them a glance that quickly turned to a cop's stare.

"You want something?" Mason asked to stop his brother from asking his own question. A question that would no doubt involve what was going on between Abbie and him.

"Yeah." And that's all Dade said for several moments while he continued to look them over. "Ace is in surgery, and the hospital will call when he's out."

Mason mentally punched himself again. Ace Chapman should have been in the forefront of his mind. Not kissing Abbie. This attraction was a distraction, and it wouldn't help him get to the bottom of what was going on.

"Why is he still here?" Dade asked, hitching his thumb in Boone's direction.

Mason could go a couple of ways with this, but he took the easy road. "He's waiting for news."

Dade's lifted eyebrow was a cue for Mason to provide more, and he would have if Grayson hadn't come up the hall.

"It's Lynette," Grayson announced. "She found something." He clicked the speaker button on his phone and lifted it for them to hear.

"I went through the probate records," Mason heard his sister-in-law say on the other end of the line. "I wasn't at the reading of the will, but my father apparently left three sealed letters in a safety deposit box in San Antonio. He also left instructions with his lawyer to hand out those letters after his death."

Beside him, Abbie pulled in a hard breath. Grayson wasn't faring much better in the breath department. Because, Mason doubted that Ford had left inspirational advice or good tiding in those sealed envelopes.

"Who got the letters?" he asked.

And Mason braced himself for news that he was certain he didn't want to hear.

Chapter Eleven

"Those letters went to Rodney Stone and Nicole Manning," Abbie heard Lynette Ryland say. "And the third went to Vernon Ferguson."

Lynette paused, no doubt when she heard their collective groans and mumbles. "Is Ferguson the man you think tried to kill the horse trainer at the ranch?"

"The very one," Grayson assured her. "Any idea what was in those letters?"

"None," Lynette quickly answered. "As I said, I didn't even go to the reading of the will, but I can ask my father's former secretary. She and I are still close, and she might have typed the letters for him."

To Abbie that sounded like a long shot. Considering the possible nature of the letters, the senator would have typed them himself. Or hired someone he could eliminate. But right now long shots were all they had.

That, and Ace.

If he survived the surgery, they might be able to get him to confess the name of the person who had hired him, and if they got very lucky, maybe he would tell them what the letter had said. Of course, Ferguson had already admitted that he knew Ford had left instructions to kill them all, so maybe the letters were just that: instructions to kill.

"What about a connection between Ferguson and your

father?" Mason asked Lynette. "Did you find anything other than this letter to link the two men?"

"Nothing so far. In fact, I just searched through the computer files I have, and Ferguson's name isn't mentioned. I'll keep digging. I don't have access to all of my father's things—he disowned me a few days before he killed himself—but before he died, I copied some of his files. *Lots of them*," she corrected. "I'll go through those now."

"Look for a connection that happened about twenty years ago," Mason added.

An uncomfortable silence went through the room, and Abbie knew why. Twenty years ago was when Boone had left and Ford had killed both Chet Ryland and Lynette's mother. The very woman who had had an affair with Boone.

It was also the year Ferguson had gunned down Abbie's own mother.

On the surface, this shouldn't be connected, but maybe she was missing something. Or someone. The only real living link to all of this was Boone himself. But certainly if Boone knew something, he would tell her, right?

But he hadn't told her about the affair. In fact, Boone had kept a lot of secrets.

Abbie quickly pushed that aside. She wouldn't doubt him, not after everything he'd done for her.

"If I find anything, I'll let you know," Lynette assured them.

"Thanks." Now it was Grayson's turn to pause. "You do know that Boone's back in Silver Creek?"

"Yes," Lynette said cautiously, as if she'd just stepped on a few eggshells. "Gage is, uh, considering what to do. I warn you, though, he's not happy about this."

The brothers exchanged uneasy glances. "Try to keep Gage away from here for a while," Grayson suggested. "A fight won't do us any good right now."

"I'll see what I can do," Lynette promised. "But Gage is, well, Gage."

Another brother. One who no doubt hated Boone as much as the others, because there was a possibility of a fight. It had already been a long morning, but it was apparently about to get a lot longer.

"We already knew that Ferguson had contact with Nicole Manning and Rodney Stone," Mason reminded them the moment Grayson ended the call. "And contact with Ford, too. It's not much of a stretch for Ford to give a lowlife like Ferguson an order to kill. Ferguson could have then hired another lowlife like Ace."

The brothers exchanged more groans. "Three letters," Dade repeated. "That means all three of the people who received them can continue to point fingers at each other."

Oh, mercy. Abbie hadn't even considered that. Maybe only one letter was a death warrant, and the other two were there just to muddy the waters. If so, it would work because no one would simply confess to conspiracy to commit murder.

Even though Abbie had never met Ford Herrington, she was getting a clearer picture of what he'd been capable of, and of course, he would attach himself to someone equally evil like Ferguson.

"I'll get Nicole and Stone back in here for questioning. Ferguson, too," Grayson insisted although he didn't sound any more optimistic than Abbie felt.

Mason looked at Abbie. "Did Ford ever contact you?"

"No." And Abbie was almost positive of that. "Twenty years is a long time. A lot of people have come in and out of our lives, but I don't remember Ford. And I think I'd remember seeing him."

Mason made a sound of understanding. *"Our,"* he mumbled.

Our as in Boone and her. Abbie wished she could take it back because the scowls returned to all of the Ryland brothers' faces.

Mason pushed past her, and with all of them following, he made his way back to the front of the building where Boone was still waiting. Boone was seated, but the moment he spotted them, he eased to a standing position.

"Something else wrong?" Boone asked. His gaze went straight to Abbie.

"Maybe." She figured this would sound better coming from her than his sons, because their scowls had returned. "You said Ford came to see you, to tell you that your wife had committed suicide. Did he see me?"

Boone scrubbed his hand over his forehead, and for a moment he looked confused. That was before the concern slashed through his eyes. "You think—" But that was as far as Boone got.

The back door flew open, the movement so abrupt that it slammed against the wall. She heard Mason mumble some profanity under his breath. Dade did, too.

And Abbie soon saw why.

It wasn't Ferguson or some gunman, but there was a threat nonetheless. She automatically stepped in front of Boone, and just as automatically, he pushed her to the side.

So he could face their visitors head-on.

MASON WATCHED AS HIS brothers walked in. First, Nate. The calm and sensible one who was also Dade's fraternal twin. Nate didn't look ready to explode. But the other two, well, that was a different story. Gage and Kade were spoiling for a fight. Lynette obviously hadn't been able to convince Gage to stay out of this.

"It's true," Gage spat out like profanity.

Mason was far from being a fan of Boone, but Abbie had already been put through too many wringers today.

That thought stopped him cold.

Since when did he react based on someone else's feelings, someone who wasn't a sibling?

Apparently now.

Because Mason maneuvered himself in front of her. In front of Boone, too, and he glared at his younger brothers—Dade included—who had already joined the battle march with the others toward the reception counter.

"I want you to leave now!" Gage punctuated that by jabbing his index finger at Boone.

"He'll leave when this investigation is over," Mason let them all know. Grayson gave a hesitant but concurring nod. "Abbie's in danger. Hell, we all are. And Boone stays put until I throw at least one dirtbag in jail for taking shots at us."

That took a little of the fighting fire out of Gage's eyes. Unlike Nate, this brother was not the calm and sensible one.

"Lynette said we could all be in danger," Gage tossed out there.

"We are," Mason verified. "Ford might have left orders to have us all killed, and Abbie might have gotten caught in the cross fire." Or she could be the reason for the cross fire, but Mason kept that to himself. This little family reunion was already complicated enough.

"I left Darcy and the kids with two of my detectives," Nate explained. "And I sent two more to stay with Lynette at the newspaper office where she's working today."

Darcy was Nate's wife and the assistant district attorney, and yeah, it didn't surprise Mason that Nate would think of them at a time like this. The Rylands were often a fiery lot, but they put their families first.

Unlike Boone.

The afterthought was still automatic, but Mason knew he was going to have to give it some thinking time. Maybe he could combine it with a cold beer and another kissing session with Abbie. Kissing her confused the heck out of things, but heaven help him, it felt good.

"Why did you come back?" Nate asked, his attention fastened on Boone. There was cool anger in his voice, but there was no mistaking the fact that it *was* anger.

Boone tipped his head to the bullet-damaged safety glass in the door. "Because of that. Because you're right about all of you being in danger." He shook his head, dipped his gaze. "I tried to stop this from happening."

His words did nothing to soothe Gage. He came closer, with Kade right on his heels. No surprise that the two were presenting a united front. Gage and Kade were the youngest of the pack and were just as much friends as they were brothers.

"Grayson called," Gage said. No coolness in his voice. "He explained what's happening."

"Ford could be behind the attack," Mason verified. He didn't owe Boone anything, but he wanted to clarify to his hotheaded brother that the person responsible for this mess wasn't in the room but rather in the grave.

"Ford," Gage repeated with even more venom. Yeah, his late father-in-law wasn't exactly a do-gooder. "That doesn't mean he should be here." Another finger jab at Boone. "He could have told us this over the phone."

Boone nodded. "I could have, but I wanted to see my sons."

Oh, man. That was *not* the right thing to say, and it

started an explosion of profanity and old-wound accusations from Dade, Gage and Kade. Mason wasn't much for a verbal brawl, especially when he looked at Abbie. She had her hands up, already posturing herself to protect Boone. But Mason noticed something else.

She was blinking back tears.

This was ripping her apart as much as it was his brothers.

"Stop," Mason said. He didn't shout. Didn't have to. For years he'd worked on his ice-man, badass facade, and times like this, it came in handy.

Everybody stopped. They stared at him. Waiting, no doubt, for some words of wisdom to make this all better. Or maybe waiting for him to toss Boone out on his ear. But wise words were Grayson's department. The tossing? Best left for Gage or Dade. Mason did what he did best. He was putting an end to this now.

"You can settle your differences with Boone later. Right now, we focus on keeping us all alive. Got that?"

They weren't pleased about it, but no brother objected. Grayson even made a sound of agreement and turned to Kade. "What about Bree and the twins? Where are they?"

Mason cursed himself for not already thinking of Kade's wife and babies. Bree was a deputy sheriff, but that didn't mean he wanted her trying to fend off an assassin by herself.

"They're okay," Kade assured him. "Bree took the twins and drove to Kayla's estate in San Antonio. Kayla has a bodyguard with them."

Good. That meant Kayla, Dade's wife, was safe, as well. Plus, the estate was more like a fortress, and they'd used it before when family members needed protection.

So that left Abbie.

Not family, exactly, but she was still in danger and

standing in front of a glass door and window where a hired gun could spot her and take aim. Ace might be out of commission, but that didn't mean Ford and/or Ferguson hadn't arranged for backup.

"I'm taking Abbie upstairs to the apartment," Mason let the others know. "She can stay there while I make some calls, check on Ace's condition, and then I'll take her back to the ranch."

As expected, that earned him a few raised eyebrows, and in return Mason's scowl deepened. He didn't bother to remind them about bullets going through glass or the tenacity of the men they were dealing with. He just took Abbie's arm and got moving.

"The apartment?" Abbie questioned, looking back at the others.

"A glorified flop room," Mason clarified. He got her past his brothers and down the hall to the back stairs. "You can get some rest there, and I'll have food brought up."

She didn't argue, which told him just how exhausted she was. He needed to make those calls fast and make sure the ranch was as secure as it could be before he drove her back out there.

They went up the stairs, and Mason threw open the door. Yeah, definitely a flop room, but once it had been the jail and storage area. Now, it was just one big room with a bed, sitting area, kitchenette and bathroom.

"Get some rest." He glanced at the bed and turned to get out of there fast. Having Abbie with him and in the vicinity of a bed wasn't a good idea.

But Abbie didn't let him leave. She stepped in front of him. "Thank you."

Mason didn't ask for any clarification because it would keep him there longer, but Abbie still didn't let him leave. She touched the seam on the sleeve of his black T-shirt and then started to run her fingers over it. Not touching *him* but still touching.

"Will you always hate me because of Boone?" she asked.

The question took him aback, not because he hadn't thought about it, but because Mason hadn't expected Abbie to come right out and ask.

"No, but I'll always *want* to hate you." He cursed, shook his head. "That's a lie. I don't want to hate you at all. I want to kiss you hard and long. And more than that, I want you in my bed."

She didn't back away, didn't stop touching his shirt. But she did dodge his gaze.

"This is the point where you want to run in the opposite direction," he suggested.

"I don't want to run." Now she looked up at him. "I want to be in your bed."

Mason cursed some more, but the profanity didn't stop the heat from just sliding hot and deep into him. Just the way he wanted to slide right into her.

"And then what?" he asked.

She gave a quick, awkward shrug. Then fought a smile. "We have sex?"

"Smart-ass," he mumbled.

But there was no anger in it. Just frustration that the bed thing couldn't happen right now. Or that it would happen despite the bad consequences. Disgusted with her, himself and this body heat, he slipped his arm around her waist and eased her to him.

That didn't help with the heat either.

"I don't usually talk this much about having sex," he snarled. "I just more or less do it."

She smiled again and, man, it was incredible. Abbie

was a knockout, and no part of him was going to let him forget it.

"I've thrown you off your game," she said, her breath making the words a whisper.

"No game," he admitted. "And that's part of the problem. It'd be easier if this could be just a one-night stand. I'm good at those."

"I'll bet you are." Her breath went even thinner, and she slipped her gaze down his chest and to the front of his Wranglers.

Mason couldn't help it. He laughed. Okay, not a laugh exactly, but it was as close as he got.

He stared at her, lifted his hand to her mouth and brushed the pad of his thumb over her bottom lip. She made a shivery sound, and her eyelids fluttered closed.

His body clenched.

Begged.

Then started to ache.

"You're overthinking this," Abbie said, melting against him until her face was cushioned right in the crook of his neck.

"Maybe you're right." He wanted her to be right. "You come to my bed tonight, and we can overthink it later." When he'd taken her hard, fast and deep.

The thought kept repeating in his head, and that was probably why he didn't hear the footsteps until they were practically right on Abbie and him. Mason swung in the direction of the doorway, automatically reaching for his gun. But it wasn't the threat that his body had prepared him for. It was just Gage. With a funny look on his face.

Mason huffed. Gage had no doubt noticed the close contact between Abbie and him, and Mason was sure he'd get an earful about it later. Heck, an earful might actually do him some good.

Might.

"What?" Mason snarled because Gage wouldn't have expected any other tone from him.

Gage hitched his thumb to the stairs. "Lynette's on the phone. And I think you'll want to hear what she has to say." Gage paused, his gaze shifting to Abbie. "She found something about *you* in her father's files."

Chapter Twelve

Abbie hated being the topic of conversation, especially when it was six lawmen doing the conversing about the memo that Lynette had found.

The memo was actually a handwritten request from Ford to the P.I. agency he used to find the identity of the "kid" living with Boone Ryland in Mesa, Texas.

That kid was Abbie.

The timing and place left no doubt about it, and it co-incided with Ford's visit to tell Boone about his wife's suicide.

Now the trick would be to find something else that would prove that Ford had not only learned her identity but that he'd reported it and her location to Ferguson.

All six Ryland brothers were at the massive wood table in the family-style kitchen at the ranch with stacks of files, papers, laptops and the remainder of brisket dinner that had been served by Bessie, the cook.

"You didn't eat enough," Bessie whispered to Abbie.

No, she hadn't, but her stomach was still churning and had been since Lynette's call earlier that day. It also didn't help that Mason and the others had devoted the entire afternoon to figuring out what Lynette had found in her father's files.

"It's okay," Lynette whispered to Abbie, and gave her a sympathetic look. "They'll get to the bottom of this."

Because Lynette had said that for the past couple of hours, Abbie had her doubts. Still, the lawmen were digging through the stacks of files that Lynette had brought over.

While she and Lynette helped Bessie with the dishes, Abbie glanced at Mason, something she'd been doing a lot. Each time his attention had been fastened to the files, but for this latest round, her glance met his. Mason didn't say a word, just made a slight shift in his expression, seemingly asking if she was all right.

Abbie settled for a nod.

Lynette made a hmm-ing sound that snagged Abbie's attention. Mason's sister-in-law hadn't missed the exchange, and judging from her slight smile, she hadn't missed the heat between her and Mason.

"Is it serious?" Lynette whispered.

"No, it's just this crazy attraction." But why had she admitted that to a woman she hardly knew? And why did it feel like a lie? Yes, the attraction was there. No doubt about it. However, Abbie was afraid this was going to lead to a massive broken heart for her.

"Gage and the others won't like it," Lynette said, still keeping her voice low. "Not at first anyway. But they'll get over it."

"Will they?" Again, she didn't think before she spoke, but Abbie wasn't surprised to realize that she really wanted to know the answer.

Lynette patted her arm, smiled softly. "They will."

Abbie had known the woman for only a few hours, but she already liked her. And hoped Lynette was right. Of course, the minute that the danger was over, Mason might insist that she leave before he and his brothers had a chance to *get over it*.

Grayson's phone rang, the sound shooting through the rumble of conversation, and he put the call on speaker after glancing at the screen.

"Dr. Mickelson?" Grayson said.

Abbie automatically held her breath because this was no doubt an update about Ace Chapman.

"No change in Chapman's condition," the doctor said. "He hasn't regained consciousness since the surgery."

Mason groaned. Abbie mentally did the same. They needed him to wake up so he could tell them who had hired him.

"It's not good," Dr. Mickelson continued. "And neither are the rest of his vital signs. I think you have to brace yourself for the likelihood that he's not going to wake up."

They'd already braced themselves for that, but Abbie couldn't give up hope.

Grayson thanked the doctor, ended the call and looked around the table. "So what do we have?" he tossed out there.

"The memo Lynette found, of course," Gage volunteered. "And confirmation that Ford paid the P.I. agency for eleven hours of work to identify the *minor child*."

"The eleven hours is proof they did just that," Mason stated. He looked at her. "Because if they hadn't, the P.I.s would have been on the assignment a lot longer."

Yes, she hadn't considered that. So Ford had learned who she was.

"Two days after the P.I.s were paid, there was another attempt to kill Abbie," Mason continued. "There's no proof that Ferguson was behind that, but..."

"There's proof," Abbie interrupted. "Ferguson left some kind of message on our answering machine."

"Message?" Gage and Mason questioned in unison.

Abbie shook her head. "Boone erased it. I heard him listening to it and I recognized Ferguson's voice. That afternoon as Boone and I were trying to leave, someone tried to kill me."

The brothers exchanged uneasy glances. "Why would Boone erase it?" Mason asked.

But Abbie had to shake her head again. "Boone must have realized there was a threat because he was trying to get me out of there fast." Then she paused. "But why would Ferguson leave a threat that would implicate him in another attempt to kill me?"

The question didn't earn her any nods or answers, but it did create some scowls and under-the-breath mumbles. Probably because this meant one of them was going to have to have a conversation with Boone. He was still in town at the hotel near the sheriff's office, but they no doubt wanted to avoid him.

"I can call him now and ask him about the message," Abbie let them know.

"No," Grayson insisted. But he didn't say anything else and that uncomfortable silence returned.

"The question should be asked during an interview," Mason finally said. "If you alert him that we know about the erased message, then it might give him time to come up with an answer."

Abbie blinked. "An answer that isn't the truth," she concluded. Now she was the one to groan.

Mason stood, sliding the papers he'd held back onto the table. "It wouldn't be the first time Boone has lied. And I know you think highly of him—"

"And I know you don't," Abbie interrupted. It took her a moment to get control of her voice. "Boone wouldn't lie about something like this, about something that could affect our safety."

None of them agreed with her. The best she got was a so-so shrug from Bessie. The coldest response was from Mason, and that's when it hit her. Lynette had been wrong. The Rylands were never going to get past this.

Never.

That little fantasy she'd been weaving in her head about Mason turned to dust. It felt as if her legs had, too.

"I think I'll turn in for the night," Abbie managed to say around the lump in her throat.

It was way too early for bed, but she figured none of them would mention that. They didn't. So Abbie got out of there as fast as she could. She mumbled a thanks to Bessie for the dinner and hurried up the stairs to the guest room where she'd slept the night before.

Abbie made a beeline for the bathroom and the shower, and she stripped off her shoes, shirt and pants. Tossed them on the floor. Just as Mason threw open the door.

He froze.

So did Abbie.

And she followed his gaze as it slid down her body. First to the silver concho pendant that must have riled every bone in his body. Then to her bra and panties.

No riled look for those.

Heat sizzled in those cool gray eyes.

"I stormed out of the kitchen," she reminded him. Abbie picked up the shirt and held it in front of her like a shield. "I figured you'd let me stew awhile."

He flexed his eyebrows, eased the door shut and leaned back against it. "If I'd let you stew much longer, I would have found you naked."

True. And the possibilities of that left her a little embarrassed—and aroused.

"Boone won't lie about the message he erased," she re-stated, just to get that out of the way.

He nodded, made a sound of agreement that came from deep within his throat. A husky male rumbling that shook her body and blood.

Abbie tried to hang on to the anger, she really tried, but it was hard to do while standing there in her borrowed ill-fitting underwear. And with Mason in the room. Especially with Mason. Every riled bone in her own body was attracted to him.

"Damn you," she grumbled.

The corner of his mouth lifted. "I feel the same way about you." He reached behind his back, locked the door and pushed himself away from it.

It was the sound of the lock clicking that caused her heart to slam against her chest, but when he made it to her, when he hooked his arm around her and hauled her to him, that robbed her of her breath.

Mason kissed her.

This wasn't the gentle kisses he'd doled out earlier. No, it was as if something dark and dangerous had been un-leashed, and he took full control. He anchored her to him with that hooked right arm, and his left hand went to the back of her neck. He angled her head so he could deepen the kiss.

Yes! That was the thought that went through her mind. The only thought that had time to form because Mason continued the assault on her mouth until thinking was next to impossible.

He dropped his hand from her neck, sliding it between them. And over her breasts. The breath she'd managed to catch vanished again, and Abbie only felt the heat. The need.

She only felt Mason.

He unclipped the front hook of her bra, and her breasts spilled out into his hands. His touch there alone was enough to make her legs go weak, but then he shoved aside the concho, lowered his head and took her right nipple into his mouth.

Abbie made a shivery sound and sagged against him. The only thing she could do was hold on for this wild ride.

He lifted her, and Abbie wrapped her legs around him to bring the center of her body right against his. The pleasure slammed through her, instant and hot, and she had no doubt that this was what she wanted. Mason wanted it, too, because he carried her to the bed and let her drop onto the soft mattress. He followed until he was on top of her and settled right between her legs.

Abbie couldn't process everything. It was coming at her so fast that all she could do was feel and let Mason take her anywhere he wanted to go.

He caught his thumb on the elastic top of her panties and shimmied them off her body. She was naked now. Not a stitch of clothing. But Mason was fully dressed, and she wanted to do something about that. She fought with his shirt while he fought to get his boots off. It was working until his hand went lower. And lower. Until he slid his fingers into her.

Abbie gasped.

The heat soared too hot, too much, too fast. The climax hit her before she had a chance to say anything. She'd expected something amazing with Mason.

But she hadn't expected *this*.

She hadn't expected for it to feel as if he'd shattered her body into a thousand pieces of light and fire.

It took her a moment to open her eyes. Another moment to catch her breath. And yet another moment to see the look on Mason's face. He wasn't touching her now. His hand had frozen in place. His mouth was slightly open. And he was staring at her, waiting.

Abbie knew exactly what he was waiting for.

"It's my first time," she managed to say.

His mouth was still open. He still had that poleaxed expression on his face, but it took a while to speak. "You're a virgin." And it wasn't a question.

She nodded. Swallowed hard. "Please tell me it doesn't make a difference." Abbie reached for him, to hold him in place so they could finish what they'd started.

But Mason moved off her and stepped away from the bed. Mumbling something that she couldn't quite catch, he started to pace.

"It doesn't make a difference," she insisted.

"To hell it doesn't." He tossed his hands in the air, palms up. "Trust me, it makes a difference."

She groaned, already anticipating the discussion—no, make that an argument—they were about to have. She got to her feet, righted her bra and put her panties back on. "It wasn't as if I planned it this way. I've been in witness protection since I was eleven. Not many opportunities came up for me to trust someone enough to hop into bed with them."

He aimed a scowl at her. "You should have told me before I ever kissed you."

Now it was her turn to scowl. "And just how would I have worked that into the conversation, huh? If I'd said I was a virgin, you would have thought I was some innocent naive woman that you couldn't touch."

"Yeah, I would have." His hands went in the air again. "And I darn sure wouldn't have kissed you, got that?"

Yes, she *got that*. On some level Abbie had known what

his reaction would be, and maybe that's why she hadn't told him. She'd wanted that kiss. She'd wanted to know what it would feel like to be with Mason—in his arms and in his bed.

Frustrated with herself and with Mason, Abbie snatched her clothes from the floor and started putting them back on. "You think having sex with me will mean a commitment."

He stared at her, gave her a flat *duh* look.

"It doesn't have to be," she assured him.

"Yeah, it does."

She caught onto his arm when he started to walk away. "Why? Because you'd be my first? Get over yourself, Mason. I'm thirty-two years old. How many women my age do you think stayed with their first lovers?"

He paused, moved in closer. "It doesn't matter." His thumb landed against his chest, and he spoke through clenched teeth. "*I* don't sleep with virgins."

She wanted to ask if that was true, if he'd ever had a virgin for a lover, but Abbie knew he wasn't lying. Mason had lived his life keeping people at arm's length, at creating this dark and brooding facade that frightened people. Virgins steered clear of him, and he did the same to them.

"Sex is simpler if there are no strings attached," Abbie mumbled.

Mason certainly didn't deny that. "And you come with plenty of strings."

Again, she could only nod and try to push aside the dull ache still burning in her body. Yes, he'd made her climax, but it didn't seem nearly enough when she was lusting after every inch of him.

Mason cursed again, making her believe that he was still doing some lusting of his own. He moved away from her, sank down onto the foot of the bed and cursed some more.

"A virgin," he said, and he repeated it. "I wouldn't have guessed."

"Then maybe I should have let you find out the hard way." Abbie gave him a flat look so that he'd know she was joking.

Well, maybe.

Mason returned the flat look. "Do I need to give you the talk about your first time being with someone special?"

"You *are* special." Abbie said it fast, like ripping off a bandage. Besides, fast meant he couldn't add anything else—like making it special with someone she loved.

The *L* word would send Mason running.

She huffed. Heck, he already was running.

Abbie went to him, despite the warning glare he gave her, and she slid her hand through his hair, tilting his head slightly so they made direct eye contact.

"I don't want you to be special. I don't want to feel this way about you. Because I know my strings complicate things." Abbie didn't back down, although this wasn't easy. "But I can't help it. I want you, and I'm possibly falling in love with you."

Let the running begin.

He huffed, stood and brushed a very chaste kiss on her cheek. "I'm not the right man for you." And with that, he started for the door. Not exactly running but close.

"Who says you're not?" she fired back.

Mason stopped, kept his back to her. "Anyone who knows me."

Abbie's hands went to her hips. "I'll venture a guess that no one knows you because you haven't let anyone in since you were seventeen."

He glanced at her over his shoulder. No scowl or glare

this time, but amusement danced through his eyes. "Analyzing me?"

The moment called for some levity. "Seducing you, but obviously failing."

Mason laughed in that low husky way that always made her melt. Oh, yeah. She was possibly falling in love with him.

He opened his mouth, but the sound stopped him from saying anything. Abbie was so focused on him that it took her a moment to realize his cell was ringing. Mason took it from his pocket, cursed.

"It's Rodney Stone," he relayed to her and answered it by putting the call on Speaker.

"I went by the sheriff's office, but none of you were there, just the night deputy, and I don't want to talk to her. She gave me your cell number."

"What do you want?" Mason demanded, the impatience evident in his voice. Abbie was right there with them. She'd had enough of all their suspects for one day.

"I want you and your brothers to investigate Nicole Manning," Stone insisted.

"We are. And you, too. In fact, we want to know what was in the letter that you got from Ford Herrington."

Silence for several moments. "The letter's not important. It was just to thank me for all my years of service."

"Admirable." Sarcasm replaced the impatience. "But I'll want to read it."

"Fine," Stone snapped. "Read it and then do your job. Investigate Nicole."

"Anything specific or are you just slinging mud?" Mason asked.

"No mud. Be at the sheriff's office tomorrow morning, and I'll bring proof."

"Proof of what?" Mason pressed when Stone didn't continue.

He made that smug sound that Abbie had heard him make earlier. "Proof that Nicole is the one who's trying to kill all of you."

Chapter Thirteen

Mason gulped his third cup of coffee while he finished up the paperwork for the arson and shooting incident at the ranch. Later, he'd have to do the same for Ace Chapman's second attack and then the reports that would come when Rodney Stone arrived with his so-called evidence. He hated paperwork and hated even more when he couldn't get his mind centered on it. And Mason knew the exact reason for his lack of focus.

Abbie.

Man, fate was laughing its butt off right about now. In high school other guys had wanted virgin trophies, but not him. He preferred his women with some baggage. Women who didn't want a commitment any more than he did. He'd steered clear of virgins, Goody Two-shoes and anyone with marrying potential.

Until now.

And he could still steer clear, he reminded himself. Maybe Ace would regain consciousness and spill all the details about who hired him. Maybe Stone could give them something to arrest Nicole. Or vice versa. Mason didn't care who was responsible, only that he wanted that person out of commission and facing down some justice. Then he could give some serious thought to this emotional mess with Abbie.

A virgin!

Well, it ruled out a one-night stand, that's for sure. Of course, that didn't stop him from wanting both her and that single encounter in bed. He huffed. No, it didn't rule out anything except he was going to have to figure out a way to keep his hands off her.

That resolution lasted about a second.

Carrying a bag from Tip Top Diner, Abbie stepped into the doorway of his office, and she looked far better than any woman had a right to look. Snug jeans that she'd borrowed from Dade's wife, Kayla. Mason never remembered those jeans looking that great on his sister-in-law. The borrowed sapphire-blue top was in the same category.

Hot.

And *hot* and *virgin* didn't go together. Not for him.

Abbie had pulled her hair back into a ponytail, something she'd likely done for comfort and not to make him notice her neck.

"Dade got us cinnamon rolls," she announced, smiling. Damn. That smile was working a number on him, too.

Abbie opened the bag, deposited one of the wrapped heavenly smelling pastries on his desk and then took out one for herself. She made an mmm-ing sound when she bit into it.

Mason's body started to beg when she licked her fingers.

Oh, this is going great.

"You're in a good mood," he settled for saying, and his tone let her know that he didn't share that mood with her. He was frustrated, ornery and in need of sex.

Hell.

He was in need of Abbie, and that only made his mood worse.

"I'm optimistic," she explained, glancing at the clock.

"Stone is due here any minute now. By lunch, we could all be out of danger."

Maybe. Mason didn't have a lot of faith in Stone. Nor their other suspects—Nicole and Ferguson. He had to add Boone's name to that list, as well. He didn't think for a minute that Boone had hired anyone to shoot at Abbie, but Mason had to ask him about that phone message that he'd erased. Boone could be some kind of unwilling or unknowing accomplice.

"Marshal McKinney called a few minutes ago," Mason filled her in. "He's still working on a new identity and location for you. He might have something ready by the end of the day and wants you to stay in my protective custody until then."

Abbie studied him a moment. "Are you scowling because of that or because of last night?"

"I always scowl," he reminded her, and he definitely didn't want to talk about *last night*.

"Not always. Sometimes, you have a back-off expression that looks like a scowl. But this one is the real deal." She didn't wait for him to comment on that observation. "So are you regretting that you didn't sleep with me, or are you just upset that things got as far as they did?"

Mason was sure he didn't want to answer that either, and that certainty went up a notch when he realized Dade was standing in the doorway. Ah, heck. He'd let Abbie's questions, tight jeans and finger licking distract him, and now his brother had overheard the questions that Mason would have preferred to keep private.

And unanswered.

Dade's eyebrow hiked up. So did the corner of his mouth. Yeah, Dade was enjoying this, and if kept enjoying it, he was about to be a dead man.

Abbie's face turned red, and she dodged Dade's gaze.

"You'd better not have anything to say. Got that?" Mason dared his brother.

Dade held his hands up in mock surrender, and he looked at Abbie. "He likes to say *got that* a lot. Have you noticed?"

She nodded. "I've been on the receiving end of a few of them. It means shut up and don't argue."

Mason didn't contradict her. That's exactly what it meant, and Dade better not press it.

But Dade only gave him a smug look. "I thought you'd like to know that Stone just walked in." The levity faded. "And Boone. Grayson's not here yet. His baby's running a slight temp, and they might have to take him to the doctor."

They would take him to the doctor, Mason mentally corrected. The baby, Chet David, was only a month old, and there was no way his big brother would put an interrogation above his baby boy.

Mason got to his feet. "Put Stone in the interview room. I'll talk to Boone here in my office." Because he didn't want another go-round in reception. Abbie would no doubt want to follow him there, and Mason didn't want her near all that glass.

"I'll send Boone back," Dade mumbled.

Abbie ditched the rest of her cinnamon roll, shoving it back into the bag, and she stood, as well. No doubt waiting for Mason to send her out of the room so he could conduct an official interview with Boone.

"You can stay," he let her know, "but I ask the questions."

She nodded and looked as if she wanted to say something. Mason only hoped it didn't have anything to do with the incident on the bed. But then she shook her head and turned toward the sound of approaching footsteps. A moment later Boone appeared in the doorway.

"Mason," he greeted. "Abbie." He didn't exactly give them the raised eyebrow as Dade had, but his forehead bunched up. Was he wondering why the two of them were together—again? No doubt. His father wasn't trustworthy, wasn't worthy of being called a father, but he wasn't stupid.

"How soon are the marshals getting Abbie out of here?" Boone asked him.

"Soon. I'm working on it. You want a lawyer present for this?"

Abbie made a slight groan, but Boone didn't look the least surprised. He just shook his head. "What's *this* about?"

Mason had no intention of soothing the concern in Boone's voice. He cut right to the chase. "When Ford visited you twenty years ago to tell you that Mom was dead, Ferguson called you shortly thereafter. You remember?"

Boone lifted his shoulder and glanced at Abbie. "What's going on?"

"You erased a message from Ferguson," she explained.

An explanation Mason didn't want her to give, but it seemed to jog Boone's memory. "Yeah, I remember." He shrugged. "Ferguson asked if Abbie was still sleeping with the lights on. Not a threat, exactly, but because he'd called the rental house, that meant he knew how to find us."

Mason felt the little twist in his stomach, and he hated that Ferguson had done things like that to Abbie. It was torture, plain and simple, and he was continuing it twenty years later.

"Any idea why Ferguson called first?" Mason asked. "If he knew where you were, why didn't he just go after Abbie without warning you?"

Boone got a pained look on his face and glanced at Abbie. "I think a man like Ferguson enjoys the hunt. And he did send someone after her. We barely made it one step out of the house when the hired gun opened fire."

"Boone had to kill the hired gun," Abbie added. "So we weren't able to prove that Ferguson hired him."

More than a twist this time. Mason's stomach turned rock hard. Abbie was alive because of Boone. No wonder she thought of him as a father.

Mason got his mind off that and back on business. "So why erase the message from Ferguson?"

"I didn't want Abbie to hear it." And Boone looked Mason straight in the eye when he answered. "Yeah, we were already in the process of leaving, but she would have taken the answering machine with us."

It was a reasonable explanation, and Mason had to remind himself that if this were any man other than Boone, he probably wouldn't have any doubts. And he had to admit that his doubts weren't even reasonable. Any fool could see that Boone loved Abbie like a daughter. So, yeah, he would have taken little steps and big ones to protect her.

Abbie gave Boone's arm a squeeze. A reassurance that she didn't share Mason's doubts.

"You two okay?" Boone asked, looking first at her and then at Mason.

She nodded. Glanced at Mason. Waiting for him to answer.

Mason figured it was a good time to change the subject. He wasn't okay. Neither was Abbie despite that nod, and he didn't want to slip into a personal conversation with a man he still hated.

"I need to question Stone. You can watch from there." Mason pointed to the room across the hall. "There's a two-way mirror."

Mason headed out fast, but before he stepped into the interview room, he took a moment to gather his thoughts and to mentally slug himself. He was lawman right now, and he had to act like one or the danger was never going to end for Abbie. With that reminder out of the way, Mason got to work.

Stone was already seated, and he had his open briefcase on the table. "Where's the sheriff?" he immediately asked.

"Busy. You get to talk to me instead." Mason spun one of the chairs around, dropped down on the seat and rested his arms on the chair back.

Stone didn't try to hide his disapproval of being relegated to an interview with a deputy, and Mason didn't attempt to hide his disapproval of a man he thought was a couple of notches below slime. Anyone who worked for Ford for two decades couldn't have stayed completely legal.

"The proof I promised." Stone took out a paper from his briefcase, reached across the table and handed it to Mason.

Mason had a good look at the *proof*. It was a lengthy email from Ford to Nicole, and the first part dealt with Ford's reelection campaign. Nothing incriminating until Mason got to the last paragraph.

"My daughter has been snooping through our old business files," Mason read. "Make sure you cover both of us. While you're at it, take care of that Ryland mess."

Mason had known that Ford's daughter, Lynette, had been looking through her father's files for proof of his wrongdoings. That fit with the date of the email—two months earlier. But Mason had to mull over what Ford had meant by the *Ryland mess*.

"Ford is telling Nicole to kill all of you, including Boone," Stone concluded.

Ford was as dirty as they came, but that interpretation was a stretch. "You have anything else?"

"Isn't that enough?" Stone howled. "Nicole is the one

behind these attacks, and she's operating on Ford's orders. He probably left her money to carry out his wishes."

That was possible, but Mason could see this from a different angle. "This might have been about the time that Ford learned my brother Gage was alive. Or he could have been referring to the fact that Lynette didn't get her marriage to Gage annulled when Ford insisted she do it."

Stone jumped to his feet. "This isn't about your brother. It's about Ford leaving instructions to have you murdered."

Mason wished that's what the email proved, but it didn't. He shook his head and dropped the paper back on the table. "I'll have Grayson look at it, but I don't think he'll come to the same conclusion you have."

Stone's hands went on his hips, and he huffed. "Somebody wants you dead, and judging from the way this investigation has stalled, that email is as close to proof as you have."

"The investigation hasn't stalled," Mason mumbled. At least he hoped not. Every passing minute meant Abbie was in danger.

Abbie. He glanced back at the mirror. She was there, watching and listening, and Mason knew it was a bad time to remember that. But each conversation about the death threats had to feel like opening old wounds, especially because this wasn't just about her. It was about all of them.

Well, not Rodney Stone.

And that brought Mason back to something else he needed to know. "What was in the letter that Ford's probate attorney gave you when the will was read?"

Stone blinked. In fact, that was his only reaction for several seconds. He obviously hadn't expected that question. "It was personal."

That wasn't the right answer. "Yeah, I bet. But considering it could be important to an attempted-murder investigation, personal doesn't count. What was in the letter?" Mason pressed.

Stone's surprise morphed into anger. "Ford thanked me for all my years of service."

Mason made a circling motion with this finger to tell Stone to keep talking.

This time Stone's eyes narrowed. "There's nothing more to add. There was no money, nothing of value. Just his thank-you for twenty-two years of putting up with him."

Okay, that little outburst seemed genuine. Of course, that could be faked. "I want to see it."

"You can't." Stone met Mason's stare. "I tore it up." He rolled his shoulders. "I was upset because I was expecting more."

"Any reason why?" Mason pressed.

"Yes!" But it took him several moments to continue. "Nicole got a letter, too, but she was grinning from ear to ear when she read hers. I'm betting Ford left her a bundle."

"Maybe. Or maybe she was grinning to rile you. If so, it worked."

Stone shook his head. "No, she was pleased about something. Maybe more orders to kill some Rylands." He cursed. "I was so mad that I ripped my letter of *thanks* into pieces and flushed it down the toilet."

"Convenient," Mason remarked.

"The truth," Stone corrected. "My letter was nothing. Less than nothing. But Nicole's, well, you should demand to see it."

Oh, Mason would, but she'd likely have the same story about getting mad and destroying it. That left Ferguson. Mason might have better luck getting a letter from a nest of rattlers.

There was a rap at the door, and a split second later, it opened. Dade stuck his head in and motioned for Mason to come into the hall. He did, bracing himself for more bad news, and he shut the door behind him.

Dade wasn't alone. Both Boone and Abbie were there, and judging from their expressions, this was going to be bad.

"Gage just called from the hospital. Ace regained consciousness," Dade immediately let Mason know.

It took a moment for the relief to set in. "Is he able to talk?"

Dade nodded. "He's not only talking but making some demands."

The feeling of relief flew right out the window. "What kind of demands?"

Dade looked at Abbie, and she was the one to answer Mason's question. "Ace told Gage that he'll speak to only Boone and me. He says if we come to the hospital, he'll tell us who hired him. *But only us.*"

"Hell," Mason mumbled, and Dade agreed. "This could be some kind of trap."

Abbie didn't argue that. "Gage said Ace is heavily sedated, and he's too weak to even get out of bed. He doesn't have a gun, and he can't hurt us."

Mason wasn't so sure of that. Maybe physically Ace couldn't do any harm, but Mason didn't trust him. If Ace was ready to confess all, then he likely had something up his sleeve.

Maybe.

Or maybe the hit man just wanted to stay alive.

"We don't have a choice," Abbie insisted.

"Yeah, we do." But Mason knew that was a lie. He wanted Abbie as far away from Ace as possible. He wanted her safe inside. Except no place was safe as long as someone wanted to kill her.

"You'll be with us," Abbie argued. "But we have to hurry. Ace said the offer is only good for fifteen minutes."

Mason cursed again. "Why the time limit?"

"Ace thinks his boss will try to kill him," Dade explained. "He wants to be moved to a more secure location ASAP."

Now, that was something Mason couldn't dispute. Ace was definitely a loose end, and the person who hired him wouldn't want him talking to anyone. Of course, getting him to a safe place wouldn't be easy.

"I'll finish up with Stone," Dade let him know. "Mel's outside in the parking lot now, just to make sure no one is out there. I'll also call Gage and have him meet you in the hospital parking lot. Kade can start working on moving Ace."

It was also his brother's way of saying for them to get to the hospital *fast*. If Ace stuck to his unreasonable condition for a confession, the minutes were literally ticking off.

Still, Mason took a moment to consider all the angles. There were some potentially bad angles in a situation like this—like the bad feeling in his gut—and it riled him to the core that he couldn't do anything about them.

"Let's go," Mason said to Abbie and Boone. He took his weapon from his shoulder holster and hurried down the hall toward the back exit. They were right behind him.

When he opened the door, he spotted Mel, the deputy, as she was canvassing the parking lot. She also had her gun drawn and gave them a thumbs-up to indicate it was safe. Well, as safe as she could make it. Mason didn't waste any time getting Boone and Abbie into his truck and out of the parking lot. Abbie slid in next to Mason, and Boone took the passenger's side.

Thankfully, Boone drew a weapon as well, his Colt, and he used the side mirror to keep watch, but he also glanced at the dash. Then at Mason. "You kept your granddaddy's truck," he commented.

"Yeah." And Mason didn't add more. It certainly wasn't the time to explain that the truck was his last thread of connection to his grandfather. It didn't mesh with the stone-hard attitude he preferred to toss back in people's faces.

Abbie leaned in a little, pressing her arm against his. "I like the truck. It suits you."

Mason frowned and wondered when the heck his choice of vehicles had become of such interest to others. But he didn't hang on to the anger long. He made the mistake of glancing down at Abbie, and he turned to dust again. That's because her eyes let him know that her truck talk was a way of calming her raw nerves.

"It'll be okay," Mason tried to assure her. He wasn't one to dole out promises he couldn't keep, but in this case he made an exception. He wanted to do something to get that worry off her face.

"What if Ace doesn't tell us what we need to know?" she asked in a whisper.

Mason lifted his shoulder, tried to look as cool and mean as possible. "Then we keep looking. Keep asking questions." Because there wasn't an alternative.

Okay, there was.

Marshal McKinney could whisk Abbie away to a new life and a new name. He could make her safe. And even though that twisted away at Mason's stomach, and even though he didn't want to explore why it was doing that, there was a bottom line here.

Abbie would be safe.

And for now, Mason would bargain with the devil to make sure that happened.

Mason pulled into the parking lot as close as he could to the entrance, and he waited until he saw Gage in the doorway before he turned off the engine. "Move fast," he told Abbie. "I don't want you outside any longer than necessary."

She nodded and followed behind him when he stepped from the truck. Mason made it just a couple of steps before he heard the sound.

And it was already too late.

A bullet slammed into his truck.

Chapter Fourteen

Abbie barely had time to react to the shot that was fired before Mason hooked his arm around her waist and dragged her to the ground.

She landed on her knees, but Mason pushed her down until she was flat against the parking lot pavement. Then he followed on top of her.

Protecting her.

Again.

"Boone?" she shouted just as another shot crashed into the window on the driver's side.

"I'm okay. Stay down!" Boone shouted back.

Abbie had no intention of doing otherwise, but she wasn't the only one in danger. Both Mason and Boone were in the line of fire, and neither would get out of that danger. And all because of her. They could die in this parking lot trying to keep her alive.

"Should I call for backup?" she asked.

Mason shook his head. "Gage will do that. Crawl underneath the truck," he ordered her.

Abbie started to do that, but the shots came at them nonstop. She also heard other shots. Not just Mason's, but ones coming from the front of the hospital where Gage was hopefully returning fire.

But who was trying to kill them this time?

It couldn't be Ace because he was in the hospital. If he'd somehow managed to escape, Gage would have told them. It wasn't Stone either, because just minutes earlier they'd left him at the sheriff's office. Of course, any of their suspects could have hired another triggerman.

Abbie rolled to the side and beneath the truck, but she still couldn't see anything because Mason adjusted his position so that he was directly in front her. She watched where he took aim and fired. Not in the parking lot or at the hospital. Mason fired the shot toward the parklike area at the back of the building.

The perfect place for a gunman to hide.

There were thick shrubs, trees and benches. So many places to lie in wait. And because the gunman had started shooting almost immediately after they'd gotten out of the truck, that meant the person had been waiting for them. Maybe that same person had used Ace's demand to put this deadly plan in motion.

"You see him?" Boone called out.

"No," Mason answered, and he sent another shot into the park. "But he's using a rifle."

Oh, mercy. So the gunman could be far enough away from them not to be spotted but still able to deliver a fatal shot.

A bullet smacked into the truck, less than an inch from where Mason had crouched.

"You need to get down!" Abbie demanded.

He didn't, of course. Mason stayed put and kept firing. Until she heard the thudding click to indicate he was out of ammunition.

"I have an extra magazine of ammo in the glove compartment," he mumbled.

Mason turned, no doubt to head in that direction, but Abbie latched on to him and pulled him back to the ground.

"Are you crazy? If the shooter's got a scope on that rifle, and he probably does, he'll pick you off the second you climb back into the truck."

Mason didn't argue. Couldn't. Because he knew she was right.

"I'm nearly out of ammo, too," Boone let them know.

That wasn't good news, but thank goodness Gage was still firing. Plus, backup should be arriving any minute.

And then Mason cursed.

Abbie's heart jumped into her throat. "What's wrong?"

"The shots are getting closer."

She listened. Hard to do with her pulse crashing in her ears, but she soon heard what Mason already had. Yes, the shots were getting closer, and that meant the gunman was moving in for the kill. But she also heard something else.

A siren.

Backup would be here soon. Hopefully soon enough.

"Crawl toward Boone," Mason told her. "I'll be right behind you."

Abbie had been about to argue, until he'd added that last part. She didn't want Mason to stay put and take a bullet. But Boone was farther away from the shots.

For now.

With the shooter moving, it was hard to know where it would be safer.

Abbie scooted to the side, toward Boone, and when she was within reach, he pulled her closer until she was tucked up against him. The shots continued—slower now but seemingly getting louder with each one fired.

Mason was just a few inches from her when a bullet cut through the front tire. The air rushed out, causing the truck to sink down right on Mason. It wasn't enough to crush him, but Abbie didn't want to take the risk. She latched on to his arm and yanked him to her.

The sound of the sirens got closer, and then Abbie heard the screech of brakes into the parking lot. She couldn't see who'd arrived to help, but she did get a glimpse of Gage.

"Stay down!" Gage yelled to them, and he barreled out of the hospital doorway.

Abbie wanted to scream for him to stay put, to keep out of the way of those shots, but just like that, they stopped.

"The shooter's on the run," Mason said, and he glanced at Boone. "Stay here with Abbie."

Before she could ask Mason where he was going or remind him that he was out of ammo, he scrambled out from beneath the truck and ran in the direction where she'd last seen Gage.

"Be careful," she called out, but it was too late for him to hear her.

Boone heard, though.

Abbie met his weathered gaze, and she saw the realization in his eyes. She had fallen hard for Mason, and it was breaking her heart to see him in danger.

"Does he know?" Boone asked her.

"What do you think?" she whispered.

Boone blew out a weary breath. Nodded. Mason didn't miss much when it came to people. Especially her. So, yeah, he knew how she felt. That didn't mean he would do anything about it or even return her feelings.

The sound of the footsteps snapped her attention back where it belonged—on the shooter and the safety of anyone who might cross his path. She prayed it was Mason returning, but she soon saw Dade.

"Get Abbie inside the hospital now," Dade told Boone. And as Gage and Mason had done, he hurried away.

Boone didn't waste any time getting her to her feet, and with his gun still drawn, he hooked his left arm around her, and they hurried up the steps to the hospital. He pushed her inside, away from the windows and doors, and stood guard in front of her. They were alone. There were others in the waiting-reception area, and they'd all taken cover behind the chairs and furniture.

Abbie came up on her toes so she could peer over Boone's shoulder. Her heart sank when she couldn't see Mason, but she knew he was trying to run down the shooter.

"Mason's out of bullets," she mumbled, causing the panic to soar.

"He knows how to take care of himself," Boone reminded her, but there was concern and fear in his voice. And there was a reason for that. Three of his sons were out there with a killer.

Another police cruiser screamed to a stop in the parking lot, and Mel made a quick exit. She, too, was armed and went in pursuit.

"They'll catch him," Boone assured her.

Abbie hung on to that, but her hopes vanished when she saw Mason making his way back through the park and toward them. Judging from his expression, the shooter was still at large.

Abbie wanted to run to Mason, to make sure he was okay, but Boone anchored her in place. She didn't fight him, not until Mason stepped inside, and then she threw off Boone's grip and ran to Mason. He caught her in his arms and pulled her to him.

"You okay?" he asked.

She nodded and checked him for any signs of injury. None, thank God. Just that look of pure frustration on his face.

"He got away?" Abbie wasn't sure she wanted to hear the answer.

The muscles in Mason's jaw flickered. "The others will keep looking."

She wanted to be strong, needed to be because Mason already had enough on his shoulders, but Abbie couldn't help it. Tears burned her eyes.

Mason mumbled something. Not his usual profanity. She couldn't make out what he said, but it soothed her more than anything else could have. So did the way he kept her cradled in his arms.

But it didn't last.

Abbie had only a few seconds of that comfort before she heard the footsteps racing toward them. Mason obviously heard them, too, because he maneuvered her behind him again. However, this wasn't a threat in the same way gunman was. It was Dr. Mickelson, and he was hurrying up the hall toward them.

"Something wrong?" Mason immediately asked the doctor.

Dr. Mickelson nodded. "I need you to come with me. *Now.*"

Chapter Fifteen

Dead.

Mason figured that wasn't the worst news he could hear today, but it wasn't good. Ace Chapman was dead. Now, not only wouldn't he get the answers about who'd hired the man, but he also had another problem. A big one.

Because Ace hadn't died of natural causes.

"Looks as if someone smothered him," Dr. Mickelson explained. His voice was shaky. Heck, he was shaky. The doc had no doubt seen death before, but murder was a whole different story.

Mason had seen death, and yeah, Ace had been smothered.

"What's going on?" Mason heard Abbie ask from the doorway of the recovery room. He'd told her to stay put, but obviously she'd followed him.

Mason couldn't blame her. This was their lives here, and they had a dead hit man and another live one loose somewhere in town. He scrubbed his hand over his face and looked back at her. Mason didn't say a word, but she must have picked up on his body language.

"Who killed him?" she wanted to know.

And Mason wanted to know the same darn thing.

He glanced around the room. No surveillance cameras here, but there was one in the hall. Not outside the door exactly, but it might have enough range to show them who'd waltzed into Recovery and put a quick end to Ace's miserable life.

"I need the surveillance disks for the last hour," Mason told the doctor.

The doctor nodded. "You can use my office, and I'll have the disk delivered there." His attention drifted to Abbie. "Might do her some good to get off her feet for a while—and get away from this."

Mason couldn't agree more, and because he couldn't take her outside with the gunman still on the loose, the hospital was the safest place to be. Hopefully.

"What should I do with the body?" Dr. Mickelson asked.

"Don't touch it. I'll call the Rangers and have them send down a CSI team. Lock this door and don't let anyone enter."

Not that he thought there was any evidence to tamper with, but they might get lucky. Still, this was likely a case of premeditated murder, so the killer had probably covered his or her tracks.

"I'll go ahead and take Abbie to your office," Mason let the doctor know.

Where he could hopefully prevent anyone else from taking shots at her. While there, he intended to arrange for someone to question their suspects—all of them—and find out if they had alibis for these latest incidents—the shooting and Ace's murder.

Mason went to Abbie, slipping his arm around her waist to get her moving. She seemed frozen, unable to take her attention off the dead assassin.

Boone was there, too, just a few feet away from her. Standing guard. Mason considered thanking him for protecting Abbie, but he wasn't feeling that generous. Besides, it was possible that Abbie was in danger because of Boone.

And if so, there went any chance of ever feeling anything but the hatred he already felt.

"Should I go to the doctor's office with you?" Boone asked.

"No need. I'll take care of her." It sounded a little like marking his territory, but Mason was too riled and weary to tone it down.

But Abbie didn't budge. "You won't go outside?" she clarified to Boone.

Boone managed to muster up a reassuring smile. "I'll stay put. Go with Mason."

She hesitated a moment, as if deciding if he was being truthful, but the adrenaline crash must have been the tipping point because she nodded and got her feet moving.

While he led her down the hall, Mason made the first call to the Rangers to request a CSI team. Grayson was still likely tied up with his sick baby, Dade and Gage were in pursuit of the gunman, so Mason went to the next on his call list. His sister-in-law Bree, a deputy sheriff and former FBI agent.

"Ferguson, Stone and Nicole will just lie and say they know nothing about this," Abbie concluded after Mason had requested that Bree reinterview all of them.

"Probably, but Bree's good at what she does. She might be able to get one of them to snap." But Mason wasn't holding his breath.

Abbie stopped cold, and her eyes widened. "Bree won't be at the sheriff's office alone with that trio of vipers?"

"Not a chance. Kade will be with her. Luis, the other deputy, too."

Relief went through her eyes. Not much, though. Probably because they didn't seem to be any closer to ending the danger.

Mason ushered her into Dr. Mickelson's office, shut

the door and tried to maneuver her to the leather sofa. But again Abbie stopped, looked up at him and then slipped into his arms. Yet another dangerous place for her to be, but judging from the small sigh she made, she didn't think so.

She was wrong.

Yeah, this felt good. Right, even. But Mason knew this holding could end with a boatload of hurt for both of them.

"I really have to figure out better coping skills for nearly getting killed," she whispered with her breath hitting against his neck.

Because he was thinking about the hurt, and the heat, it took him a moment to realize she was talking about the shooting and not this latest hugging session.

"No one has coping skills like that," he assured her.

"You do," she challenged.

"Not a chance." Especially not where Abbie was concerned. Yeah, he'd been in danger before, but this was as bad as it got. Because it involved her.

And Mason wasn't about to give that further thought.

He pushed the wisps of hair from her face and pressed a chaste kiss on her forehead. Well, it was meant to be chaste, but it turned out to be a green light for Abbie to move even closer. Until she was smashed right against him.

"I'm not a real virgin, you know," she mumbled.

Mason felt the sucker punch of surprise, and he leaned back a little so he could see her face. "Excuse me?"

"I mean I'm not naive or innocent. Over the years I've made out with guys. I just didn't get to the big finale with any of them."

"Really." And Mason was more than sure he didn't want to hear the details. Ditto on that part about not giving th[...] any further thought either.

"Really," she insisted. "I know the timing sucks for th[...]

conversation, but I can't seem to find a peaceful moment to have a heart-to-heart with you."

She had a point there. They hadn't had much time for sleep, much less conversation. Yet they'd managed to fire up this attraction to a very uncomfortable level.

"Marshal McKinney will have a new name and place for you soon," Mason reminded her. While he was at it, he reminded himself of that, too.

Abbie shook her head. "I'm not going."

That was a couple of rungs up from a sucker punch. "What?"

"I'm not going," she calmly repeated. She stepped back, hiked up her chin. "Because wherever I go, the danger will just follow. I'm tired of running, tired of being scared. I'm making my stand right here in Silver Creek."

But then her eyes widened. "Oh, God. I can't do that, can I? Because it'll put you and your family in more danger."

"We're already in *more* danger," Mason reminded her. "And if you leave, that won't stop."

There. That was his argument for her staying. And it was a good argument, too.

Mason didn't have time to dwell on things because his phone rang. He glanced down at the screen, hoping it was Dade or Gage calling to say they'd captured the shooter. No such luck.

"Ferguson," Mason answered. Because Abbie was already trying to listen, he put the call on Speaker and hoped this moron didn't say anything to add to her already-too-high stress and adrenaline levels.

"I just heard about the shooting," Ferguson greeted. "Are you all right?"

"Peachy. Did you hire this guy to kill us?" Mason demanded right off the bat.

"Of course not. I keep telling you that I wish none of you any harm. When are you going to believe me?"

"When hell freezes over." And even that wouldn't do it. Ferguson was at the top of his suspect list. "Why are you calling me?"

"Because your sister-in-law just phoned and said I was to report to the sheriff's office for an interrogation and I'm to produce the letter that Senator Herrington left me."

"Why are you calling me?" Mason repeated. "If Deputy Bree Ryland told you to do those things, then you should be busting your butt to get it done. Unless you got something to hide."

"Nothing," Ferguson calmly said. "But there's a problem with the letter." He made a sound of disappointment mixed with frustration. Both exaggerated. Both fake. "I seem to have misplaced it."

Abbie huffed. Mason didn't even bother. He'd expected it. "We'll get a search warrant to look for it." Although if there was anything incriminating in that letter, then it was ash by now or else tucked away from the reach of a search warrant.

"No need. You can search my house anytime you like. Bring Abbie. You can both look."

Oh, yeah. As if that would happen. "What did the letter say?"

"Ford just wanted to thank me for my unwavering friendship." It sounded rehearsed. Probably was.

"You're sure he didn't ask you to put hits on all of us?" Abbie asked.

"Positive." With just that one word, the smugness was crystal clear in Ferguson's voice. Maybe he was just happy that he was able to torture Abbie a little bit more. "And even if I had, I would have declined. I don't blame you for your mother's sins."

No smugness in that last comment. It sounded, well, genuine. Of course, this was Ferguson, and he was a lying expert.

"Go to the sheriff's office," Mason told the man. "Don't keep my sister-in-law waiting."

The moment that Mason hit the end-call button, the door flew open. Abbie and he automatically flew apart as if they'd been caught doing something wrong, but it wasn't one of his siblings or Boone to cast a disapproving eye. It was Dr. Mickelson, and he held up a shiny silver disk.

"Here it is," the doctor announced.

From the surveillance camera no doubt. Mason certainly hadn't forgotten about it, but he'd had another lapse of focus because he couldn't get his mind and body off Abbie.

The doctor went to his desk and put the disk into his laptop. It took only a few seconds for the images to appear on the screen, and Mason wasn't disappointed. There was a clear angle of the recovery room where Ace had been murdered.

"I talked with the security guard," the doctor said as they watched. "And he moved to the front of the building when the shots started. He doesn't remember seeing anyone specific in the area of the recovery room."

Yeah, and that made Mason suspicious. Had those shots been fired to distract the guard and them so someone could kill Ace? If so, it'd worked.

Well, maybe.

There was no audio on the surveillance footage, but Mason saw the exact moment the shots started. The people in the hall began to run and scramble for cover. The seconds ticked off slowly until someone finally came into view.

The person paused at the top of the hall, glanced around and then walked forward.

"Who is it?" Abbie asked. She moved closer to the screen until Mason and she were shoulder to shoulder.

He shook his head, not sure who they were seeing on the screen because the person was wearing a baseball cap slung low enough to cover the forehead and the eyes. Whoever it was, he or she had attempted a disguise, which meant this probably wasn't a social call.

Mason watched, waited and finally the person stepped into view.

"Hell," he mumbled. And Mason reached for his phone.

ABBIE STARED AT THE WOMAN on the other side of the two-way mirror. Nicole didn't exactly look pleased about being escorted into the sheriff's office to answer some questions. But then, Mason didn't look pleased either, as he showed her the surveillance footage from the hospital.

"Oh, God," Nicole said when she saw herself on the screen. "It's not what you think."

Mason gave her one of his best glares. "Then you tell me what's going on—other than the obvious. Why did you kill Ace Chapman?"

"I didn't kill him." And as if on cue, Nicole began to cry. "I was set up to make it look that way."

That didn't help Mason's glare. "Of course you were."

Abbie heard a sound of mock agreement that mimicked Mason's, and she looked in the doorway to see Gage standing there. Uh-oh. She wasn't up to another round with a Ryland out to bash Boone.

But Gage didn't bash. He strolled closer and watched his brother and Nicole. "She's a natural-born liar."

Abbie couldn't argue with that. Nor could she be sympathetic to Nicole's nonstop tears. The woman was crying so hard that she couldn't speak. Abbie was too tired to have anything delay this interrogation and possible arrest

Gage seemed disgusted with the display. "Rusty Burke just called and asked to speak to Mason. I guess Mason has his phone off for this little chat with Nicole."

That got Abbie's attention off Nicole. Rusty was the ranch hand who assisted her with the cutting horses. "Is something wrong?"

"Not really. Rusty's just having trouble with the new paint mare and wants Mason's okay to get rid of her."

"No," Abbie blurted out. She huffed. "The mare just needs some extra time and training, that's all. And Rusty's too timid with her."

Abbie suddenly felt stupid and overly emotional, like Nicole. Considering everything else going on, it was small potatoes, but she wished she had some time to spend with the mare. With any of the horses. Actually, she just wanted to do something normal again.

Gage stared at her. "For the record, I don't blame you for anything Boone's done." He paused. "But it's hard."

"I know," she admitted and moved on to another thought that she was overly emotional about. "I wonder if Mason will ever move past it."

He made a sound that could have meant anything. "Mason's a complex man." Gage went closer, propped a shoulder on the glass. "Does he know how you feel about him?"

Abbie opened her mouth. Closed it. Decided she'd already overshared too much in the emotion department. "That's a trick question."

"Could be," Gage admitted. "And unlike Nicole, you're not a natural-born liar, so you can't look me in the eye and say you don't have feelings for him."

He was right, and it was clear he wasn't going to leave until she gave him an answer. Abbie shrugged. The answer was obvious anyway. "I do have feelings for him."

It was an ill-timed confession. She realized that when

she looked past Gage and saw Mason. Standing there in the doorway. Listening to them. She snapped toward the mirror again and saw Nicole alone in the interview room.

"I needed to get some tissues for Nicole," Mason said. But he didn't budge. He looked first at Abbie. Then at his brother.

"Opening cans of worms?" Mason asked Gage.

Gage grinned. "Nope. Doing you a favor. And I'll do you a second one. Let me take a stab at Weeping Willow in there. You stay here and keep Abbie company. It appears y'all have some things to discuss."

He didn't wait for Mason to agree. Gage waltzed out, but not before Mason called him a smart-ass.

Abbie frowned. "I do have feelings for you," she repeated. "And I don't think you should get rid of the paint mare despite what Rusty thinks."

Mason blinked. With reason. She'd just tossed both apples and oranges at him when his mind was clearly on Nicole's interrogation.

Or maybe not.

"I never said I didn't have feelings for you," he grumbled. He crammed his hands in his jeans pockets and watched as Gage strolled into the interview room. "It's just that I'm not the marrying kind."

Abbie looked at him as if he'd sprouted horns. "You marry all the women you sleep with?"

"No." He slid her one of his glares. "But you're different, and you know it."

No, she didn't. "Different how?" she pressed.

But Mason didn't have time to answer. That's because Gage dropped down across from Nicole and started the interrogation. "Who are you claiming set you up?" Gage demanded.

"I don't know." Nicole shook her head, cried some more

"I got a phone message, and the person said he was Ace Chapman and that he had something important to tell me. He asked me to come to the hospital."

Suddenly the tears stopped, and Nicole's head whipped up. She riffled through her purse, grabbed her phone and handed it to Gage. "Here, listen for yourself. The message is still there."

Gage did listen, but he didn't seem convinced that Nicole was telling the truth. "When you got this call, Ace was recovering from surgery. You didn't think it was suspicious that he'd be calling you?"

"No. He was very convincing. And besides, I've never spoken to him, so I didn't know it wasn't his voice."

When Gage just gave her a flat look, more tears came, and Nicole buried her face in her hands.

"You're different," Mason mumbled, getting back to Abbie's earlier question, "because you get under my skin." His glare morphed to a frown. "And what about the paint mare?"

"Rusty called and wants to get rid of her. I vote no on that. I can work with her…" She stopped. "If people will quit trying to kill me."

Mason eased his gaze to hers. Stared. And then the corner of his mouth lifted. He leaned in and brushed a kiss on her forehead. "Yeah, you're different." And he turned his attention back to the interview.

Abbie didn't want to let the conversation drop, but she had no choice—because of Gage's next question.

"Did Ford leave orders for you to eliminate all the Rylands and Abbie Baker?" he asked.

"No, of course not," Nicole jumped to answer. But then she stopped, shook her head. "Ford wanted all of you dead, I won't deny that. He used to say that if anything happened to him, the Rylands would be behind it and he'd made sure that all of you would pay."

The admission chilled Abbie to the bone. Yes, Ferguson had said that Ford wanted them dead, but this was confirmation that it'd been more than just talk.

"Who would do the paying?" Gage pressed.

"I don't know. That's the truth," she added when Gage huffed. "I do know that Ford kept tabs on Boone all these years."

Gage held up his hand in a wait-a-second gesture. "Ford knew where he was?"

"Yes. Ford said it was the only way to make sure Boone didn't come back to Silver Creek. That was their deal, for Boone to stay away."

"And he had," Gage verified. "Until now. But he wasn't in Silver Creek for the first attack and the fire at the ranch."

True. Boone had been miles away. So his return hadn't been the trigger for that attempt to kill her.

"Ford knew about Abbie, too," Nicole continued. That grabbed Abbie's attention. "He always said if necessary he could use Abbie to keep Boone cooperating."

"Use her how?" Gage asked.

Nicole met his gaze. "How do you think? You knew Ford, and he wasn't a Boy Scout."

Oh, mercy. Ford would have hurt her to make Boone toe the line. It gave her the creeps to think that both Ford and Ferguson had been watching and waiting all these years.

Gage leaned forward, put his elbows on the table. "Tell me about the letter you got at the reading of Ford's will."

"That," Nicole spat out. No more hunched-over shoulders. She sat up soldier-straight. "I'm not going to let you use that letter to arrest me for these attacks. Ford might have tried to blackmail me, but that doesn't mean I've done anything wrong."

Abbie didn't know who was more surprised—Gage, Mason or her. It was the first time any of their suspects had admitted that Ford had left criminal instructions in those letters. Of course, Nicole might be lying, Abbie reminded herself, but she wanted to hear the rest of what the woman had to say.

Gage made a keep-going motion with his index finger.

"Ford was a pig," Nicole snarled. "After all those years of working my butt off for him, he writes those three stupid letters, and he puts conditions on what he'd always promised he would give me."

"What conditions?" Mason mumbled at the exact moment that Gage asked Nicole the same thing.

Her eyes widened, as if she'd said too much. But there was still a hefty dose of anger there, too. Again, maybe it was fake. Hard to tell with Nicole.

"Did you ask Ferguson and Stone about this?" she tossed back at Gage.

"We did. Both said the letters weren't important."

The sound she made was part huff, part laugh. "Right. And I invented the internet." She got to her feet. "You want to know what Ford asked us all to do? Well, this is your lucky day, Deputy Ryland. I'll call my lawyer now, and within an hour he'll make a trip to one of my safety deposit boxes, and you'll have the letter I got from Ford."

Gage stood, too. "You can tell me now what it says."

Nicole shook her head. "Best to read it for yourself, and then you'll know why Ferguson and Stone lied."

Chapter Sixteen

Mason tossed the copy of the letter onto the desk in his room. The one that Nicole's attorney had delivered to the sheriff's office earlier. He'd read it so many times that the words were burned into his memory, but it was the bottom line of that letter that turned his stomach.

And that bottom line was money.

Ford had set up a forty-million-dollar offshore account, and the money would be paid to the person who delivered eight death certificates to Ford's attorney in the Cayman Islands. Death certificates for Mason, his five brothers, Boone and Abbie. There was even an order for them to be killed.

Abbie first. Then Grayson and his brothers. And finally, Boone.

Forty million was a lot of reason to kill.

But Ferguson probably hadn't needed the money as an incentive. Maybe not Nicole either. Despite all those tears during the interview, Mason suspected she'd been in love with Ford. How far would she go to carry out his dying wishes? But then, Mason could say the same for Rodney Stone, who'd been one of Ford's confidants and friends for years.

Mason understood why the Rylands were on that hit list, but he could only speculate as to why Abbie had been included. Maybe Ford considered her Boone's daughter. Or maybe Ford had wanted Boone to have to endure losing everyone he'd loved and once loved.

That sure didn't help the uneasy feeling in his gut.

Mason got up from the desk and headed for the shower. It was much too early for bed, not even 7:30, and too late for a ride to try to burn off some of that uneasiness. He felt like a powder keg ready to go, and it was best if he avoided everyone and everything.

The ranch was locked up tight. Every part of the security system was armed. And the ranch hands were standing guard. In other words, he'd done everything except figure out who'd taken Ford up on that offer to kill. More important, he hadn't figured out how to stop that SOB from killing Abbie.

Mason got in the shower, the water way too hot to be soothing, but he needed the heat to unknot the muscles in his neck and back. He needed other things, too.

Specifically, Abbie in his bed.

But it would be stupid for him to go to her room just across the hall. He knew that. His body knew that. Heck, the state of Texas probably knew it, but the ache still settled hard and hot inside him.

Cursing the ache and himself, he finished the shower and dried himself. While still scrubbing the towel over his wet hair, he stepped into his bedroom.

And came to a quick stop.

At first he thought he was hallucinating, that maybe the ache in his body had caused him to see Abbie in his room. Not naked as in his fantasies, but close. This mirage, or whatever the heck she was, was wearing a thin white dress, and she had her back anchored against his closed door. Some hallucination.

But then he caught her scent.

Hallucinations didn't smell that good.

It was Abbie all right.

"It's a bad time for you to be here," he snarled.

She ran her gaze down the length of his body. "That depends." She stayed put, watching him. "Are you going to make me leave?"

He should do just that. *Should*. But he knew that wasn't going to happen. He was going to screw things up beyond belief, and he would probably enjoy every minute of it.

Mason huffed, tossed the towel on the floor and walked to her. He should act like a gentleman and give her another chance to come to her senses and change her mind. He didn't do that either. He made it to her, hooked his hand around the back of her neck and snapped her to him.

Abbie did her own snapping.

Her arms coiled around him, and their mouths met. Man, did they. It wasn't a kiss exactly. More like a battle, and for some reason he couldn't make his mouth and hands be gentle. Abbie needed gentle. But then, she needed a better man than him. Too bad he was what she was going to get.

Mason kissed her hard and deep until they were both starved for air. And for each other. Of course, the starving for each other had started days ago, so it didn't need much fueling. Still, they added fire to fire when he lowered his mouth to her neck. Then her breasts.

He cursed the dress. Yeah, it wasn't much of a barrier, but it had to go. Mason stripped it off over her head and found a nearly naked, warm and willing woman underneath. He pulled off her bra and panties and tried those breast kisses again and took her nipple into his mouth.

She froze, made a sound of pure pleasure.

"Breathe," he reminded her. Reminded himself, too.

"I don't want to breathe. I want you." Her voice was all silk and sex.

"Yeah, I want you to want me. But we have to slow things down."

She didn't listen. Abbie unfroze, breathed and lifted herself to hook her legs around his waist. Oh, man. Sex against sex, and he was already hard as stone. If she changed the angle just a little, then that technical virginity was gone.

Abbie moved, changed the angle.

Of course she did.

Mason heard himself curse before the fireworks exploded in his head, and that hard-as-stone part went right into her with far more force than he'd intended. Yeah, fireworks all right and blinding, knee-weakening pleasure.

Abbie gasped, the back of her head hitting against the door.

That cleared his mind. Mason continued to curse, tried to apologize, but her gasp of pain, surprise or whatever the heck it'd been, turned to another sound. This one he had no trouble identifying.

It was a low moan of pleasure.

And more. That sound seemed to vibrate through her. Through him. Then she started to move.

The fireworks rifled off again, and he knew he was working on a thread of willpower. He couldn't take her against the back of a door, so Mason caught onto her hips to stop the blinding thrusts of her lower body, and he carried her to the bed. The moment he dropped her on the mattress, she tried to pull him back on top of her.

"Hold that thought a second," he insisted, and he reached for the nightstand drawer for a condom.

She didn't hold anything. Abbie was bound and determined to finish this in record time. Mason wanted to finish it, too, but he was already screwing up enough tonight without adding unprotected sex to the mix.

"I want you," she repeated at the end of one of those purrs.

"Yeah," Mason settled for saying.

It was another battle to get the condom on, and while he fumbled—something he hadn't done since he was sixteen—Abbie drove him crazy with some touches and kisses.

"Make the ache go away," she whispered.

For a moment he considered that might be a real ache, not one fanned by the need. But nope, it was need. Because the moment he had the condom in place, she drew him right back between her legs, lifted her hips and took him into her.

She looked at him, met his gaze. "It's better than I thought it'd be."

Unfortunately, Mason felt the same, and that was saying something because his expectation had been a mile high.

He was in big trouble here.

Trouble that got worse because he didn't just have sex with her. He kissed her. Tasted her. Gathered her into his arms. He forced himself to slow down. To savor every moment of this. Because in the back of his mind he had to admit he'd never felt this way and might never feel this way again.

Abbie did some savoring of her own. She slid her legs around him, using the strength of her toned muscles to thrust him deeper inside her. The purr became a throaty moan. Her hands pressed harder. Her embrace, tighter.

Mason knew she was close and wanted to ease back to make it last, but this wasn't something that could go on very long. Not with the ache burning them both. So he gave her what she needed. He slid his hand between their bodies.

And he touched her.

Abbie gasped again. Not from pain. The climax rippled through her. Through Mason. She fought, twisted, dug her nails into his back and did the only thing her body could do when past the point of no return.

She let go.

Mason didn't even try to fight it. But in that second when he was so near the snap in his head and in his body, he made the mistake of looking at her. At her sweat-dampened face. At her wide, surprised eyes fixed on him. At her mouth that he'd kissed too hard and fast.

At *her*.

And it was Abbie's face so clear in his mind that sent him falling. He was too far gone to speak, to do anything but fall. However, that didn't stop him from hearing Abbie.

"I love you," she whispered.

Chapter Seventeen

Abbie immediately felt the change in Mason. His grip loosened, and his lax muscles went stiff. She hadn't even allowed him a second to enjoy the climax of great sex before she'd no doubt ruined everything.

"I'll be back," she managed to mumble.

Mason didn't stop her. In fact, he rolled to the side, and Abbie scooted off the bed. She grabbed her clothes, slipped on the dress and got the heck out of there.

I love you?

Abbie might as well have taken a hammer and hit Mason in the head. Talk about the worst possible thing she could say. And the really bad part?

It was true.

She did love him, but that didn't mean he had to hear it. How she felt about him was her problem, not his, and she should have just kept her big mouth shut.

Abbie hurried back into the guest room, but she didn't stop. She had to keep moving. Had to do something to ease the smothering pain in her chest.

Oh, yes. Here was that broken heart that she'd been dreading.

She washed up, dressed in the borrowed clothes—jeans, dark red shirt and boots—and stormed out of the room. Down the stairs. And she would have raced right out the door if one of the ranch hands hadn't been standing in front of it. She didn't know his name, but he had a rifle clutched in his hands. Abbie hadn't forgotten the danger, but that was a clear reminder of it.

"I need to check on one of the horses," she insisted.

He hesitated but then nodded. "I'll call Rusty and let him know you're on the way out."

Better Rusty than one of Mason's brothers. Especially Gage. He already knew about her feelings for Mason, and he would have probably seen the panic on her face.

Abbie waited impatiently for the ranch hand to disengage the security system. The moment he did that, she was out of there, on the porch and then in the yard.

It wasn't late and with the nearly full moon and security lights, she didn't have any trouble following the path. Or seeing yet another armed ranch hand. Once she was past him, Abbie broke into a run and was practically out of breath by the time she reached the stables. And a waiting Rusty.

"Does Mason know you're out here?" Rusty immediately asked.

"I'm just checking on the mare you told Gage about," she said, dodging his question.

And thankfully the mare was inside and not out in the corral or pasture. Yes, she needed some air, some space, but she didn't want to risk being gunned by whoever had taken Ford up on his beyond-the-grave wish to have them all killed.

Abbie grabbed a carrot from the treat bin, something she wouldn't have normally done. Rewarding a horse who hadn't performed well was never a good idea. But then, she was apparently in a rule-breaking mood right now.

I love you.

Those three little words had sealed her fate and meant

she'd lost Mason forever. He'd made it so clear that he wasn't the commitment type. Heck, neither was Abbie. That's one of the big reasons why she'd stayed a virgin. Until tonight. Tonight had changed everything and not for the good.

She walked the length of the stable to the last stall, where she spotted the mare. All in all, it was a good place to do some thinking. The back stable doors were partially open to allow the crisp night breeze to flow inside. Abbie could look out at the moonlit pasture while staying hidden. And under guard. Rusty kept his distance, but he didn't budge, and like the other ranch hands, he was armed with a rifle.

"Rusty said you're causing trouble." Abbie offered the mare the carrot, which the horse immediately gobbled up. "Well, knock it off."

The mare snorted, but it didn't sound like much of an agreement. Abbie sighed, leaned against the wooden stable door and tried not to fall apart. She was failing big-time and on the verge of tears when she heard the footsteps and the too-familiar gait.

Mason.

He was walking slowly, deliberately, but he was coming toward her. Maybe to give her the boot. After all, he was her boss. Abbie preferred that to the alternative—a discussion about the *I love you.*

Mason, however, didn't say a word. He just kept walking until he reached the mare's stall, and he stopped right next to her. Abbie waited. And waited. But Mason just stuck his hand through the gate to stroke the mare.

"I figured you'd be running for cover," she finally mumbled when she couldn't take the silence any longer.

Mason took his time answering. "It appears I wasn't the one doing the running."

That snapped her gaze to his. "You can't be saying you're happy about what happened." Specifically about what she'd said.

"No." He drew out the word. "But I didn't figure running would help. I can admit when I've screwed up."

So there it was. His confirmation that it'd all been a big mistake. And although it was exactly what Abbie had expected, it still stung.

"I went to your bedroom," she reminded him. "I seduced you."

His eyebrow lifted, and he gave her the look that only he and the world's greatest skeptic could have managed. "If I hadn't wanted to get you in that bed, it wouldn't have happened." Another pause. His mouth tightened. "I didn't want to hurt you, though."

"You didn't," she lied. Except it wasn't even a lie. She'd hurt herself. Mason had spelled out the rules right from the beginning, and she'd still jumped in headfirst.

"I hadn't expected it to be, well, *wow*," she mumbled.

He flinched. "I'm not sure if that's an insult or not," he mumbled. "Because I always aim for wow."

She fought a smile, mainly because this wasn't a smiling moment. Abbie gave her feelings some more thought and came to a frustrating decision. If she had to do it again, she wouldn't change a thing.

"I love you," she repeated.

He stared at her, cursed and stared some more.

"And I don't expect you to do anything about it," she snapped. "Got that?"

It was a good exit line, and one of Mason's favorite shut-up-and-quit-arguing sayings, but it would have been better if she could have exited. But when she tried to storm off, Mason caught her by the arm. He did more of the staring. More cursing, too, and then he let go of her.

"I can never give you what you want," he said.

It took a moment for the words to sink in. Well, this wasn't the big surprise she was hoping for. The change of heart that she knew was a total long shot anyway. This was Mason being Mason, and if a woman played with fire, she should expect to get burned.

Because she was mad at herself, and at him, and because she was feeling ornery, Abbie came up on her toes and kissed him. "Never is a long time, Mason."

There. Now, that was an exit line. But once again, it didn't happen. That's because Mason's phone rang. And even though she'd already started to walk away, Mason's question stopped her in her tracks.

"Who is this?" he demanded.

Abbie turned and saw his expression go from the question to the concern. No, make that fear.

"What happened?" Mason asked, his voice louder now.

Abbie could only stand there and wait. It seemed to take forever, but Mason finally pressed the end call button and then jabbed another on the keypad.

"What's wrong?" Abbie asked.

Mason just shook his head. "The killer has Grayson's wife and baby."

"How the hell did this happen?" Gage demanded the moment he stepped foot inside the ranch house.

Mason didn't fill his brother in as he'd done the others when they'd arrived in the family room. He let Kade give Gage the details so that he and Grayson could work out what needed to be done.

The ranch house was chaotic with all the brothers and their spouses present and everyone talking at once. Everyone trying to figure out how to rescue Eve and baby Chet. There was just one big problem—they didn't know where the kidnapper was holding them. And that problem was what had put the haunting look in Grayson's eyes. Thank God the other children and their nannies had all gone upstairs, because this wasn't something Mason wanted his nephews and nieces to witness.

"I shouldn't have left them in that hospital room," Grayson repeated.

"Hindsight's twenty-twenty," Mason reminded him. "You had no idea this was going to happen."

Especially because Grayson's mind had been on his sick baby. Dr. Mickelson had wanted to keep baby Chet overnight for observation, and both Eve and Grayson had stayed by his side. Until a nurse had come running into the room to tell Grayson that Mel had phoned the hospital to tell them that Gage had been shot.

"No cell reception in the hospital," Grayson repeated.

And that's why he'd run outside to call and verify what'd happened. When he realized it was a ruse, a fake call, it'd been too late. Eve and Chet had been taken. No one had seen anybody or anything.

"The killer will make some kind of ransom demand," Mason reminded his brother. "He or she doesn't get paid to hurt Eve or the baby. This is just to draw us out."

"Draw *me* out," Abbie corrected. She was standing in the doorway, her hand gripping the jamb. Probably because she wasn't too steady on her feet. "I'm the first name on Ford's death list. I'm the one the killer wants."

"You don't know that," Mason fired back. But no one agreed with him. They couldn't. Because Abbie's name was first.

She let go of the jamb, walked closer, her gaze nailed to Mason's. "When he or she calls, I'll be the ransom demand."

"To hell you will." Mason went to her, grabbed her by

the arm and pulled her out into the foyer. Of course, the nearly dozen Rylands and Bessie quit talking and focused on Mason and her.

"If you go to meet this SOB, he or she will kill you," Mason clarified, in case she hadn't understood his objection.

"And if I don't go, he might hurt Eve and the baby." She glanced over Mason's shoulder to address Grayson.

"The killer might do that anyway," Grayson admitted.

And Mason hated that he couldn't control that, that he couldn't stop it from happening. But what he could do was prevent Abbie from making herself a sacrificial lamb.

She tipped her head to the equipment bag that Nate had brought with him. A bulletproof vest was lying on top of it. "I could wear that and go in armed. You and the others could be at a safe distance. Then, when Eve and the baby are away from there, you could get me out, too."

"Yeah, with lots of bullets flying. That's not going to happen."

His cell phone rang, the sound shooting through the otherwise-silent room. *Unknown Caller* flashed across the screen, and he knew before he answered that this was the killer.

"I'm sending you a picture," the person immediately said. It was a man, but Mason didn't recognize the voice. But it could be the person who'd fired the shots at the hospital.

Mason put the call on Speaker so he could watch the image load. The others huddled around him to do the same. When the picture was ready, Mason's heart dropped to his knees. He'd hoped and prayed that all of this could be explained away.

But no.

The picture was of Eve cradling her sleeping son in her arms while a man had a gun pointed at her head.

Grayson cursed. "If you harm either of them—"

"I have no intention of hurting them," the man interrupted, "unless you give me a reason to do that."

"Where are you and what do you want?" Mason demanded. Beside him, Kade used his own phone to snap a picture of the image of Eve with her captor. No doubt to put it through the FBI's facial recognition software, because he went running toward his laptop.

Mason studied what he could see of the photo. Eve looked unharmed and was wearing a bulky down jacket that she'd used to tuck the baby inside. Good thing. Because Chet had a fever, the chilly night air wouldn't help.

"My demands are simple," the man on the phone continued. "I want each of you to come to me. I'll give you the location later, but the first person I want to see is Abbie Baker."

All eyes went to Abbie, and other than a slight intake of breath, she had no reaction. She'd already resigned herself to the demand, and that meant Mason had to change her mind. And the snake who was holding his sister-in-law and nephew.

"Having Abbie won't get you Ford's money," Mason pointed out. "Start with me and work your way down the list."

"Tempting," the man said, with sarcasm dripping from his voice. "But Ford's instructions were specific. Abbie first. The sheriff. Then you."

So it was about the money. Mason hadn't thought otherwise, but it sickened him to hear it spelled out. "We can pay you whatever Ford arranged in his will."

"Perhaps, but I have to decline. My boss says it's imperative that Ford's wishes be carried out. And here's how.

Abbie will leave *alone* and walk to the end of the ranch road where someone will pick her up. If she's followed or has anyone with her, Eve and the baby will be the ones who pay the price for you not following orders."

The color drained from Grayson's face. Mason was sure he wasn't faring much better. It sickened him to think of an innocent baby caught in the middle of all of this.

"Why does Abbie have to go alone?" Grayson pressed. "The goal is to kill all of us."

"My boss wants you to arrive one at a time. I'm not sure why exactly, and with what I'm getting paid, I'm not going to ask. All will be revealed when you need to know."

And with that, he ended the call.

Mason expected a flurry of questions and discussion, but everyone remained silent. And everyone continued to look at Abbie. She was no doubt about to remind them that she had volunteered to go, but Kade spoke before she could.

"I'm running the picture now," he explained, and that sent Gage and Nate heading in the direction of the computer. Grayson turned to go there as well, but his cell buzzed.

"Is it the kidnapper?" Mason questioned.

Grayson shook his head, answered the call on speaker. "Boone, this isn't a good time."

"I know." Boone's voice was barely a whisper. "An armed man has Eve and the baby."

Hell. What was going on now? And how the devil had Boone gotten involved?

"How do you know that?" Grayson asked, and yeah, he was suddenly suspicious.

"Because I'm looking at them now."

Mason snapped his gaze toward the phone and listened.

"Are they okay?" Grayson asked. "Have they been

hurt?" He was on the verge of panicking, and Mason doubted he could do anything to calm him down.

"They look fine. The baby's asleep, and Eve's just sitting there. The gunman is right behind her."

"Why are you there?" Mason wanted to know.

"It's not by accident. About a half hour ago, I got a call from a man who told me that if I'd come to the Ryland family cemetery, he'd let Eve and the baby go," Boone continued. "I parked my truck up the road and walked here, so I could see what was going on."

"Where are they?" Grayson demanded.

"By your mother's grave. But don't come," Boone insisted. "Not just yet. The place has been booby-trapped. I can see wires on the ground, and I'm pretty sure those wires lead to some explosives."

Not good. That made a sneak attack a whole lot harder. Not impossible, though. Somehow, they had to figure out how to do this.

Grayson had such a tight grip on the phone that Mason was surprised it didn't shatter in his hand. "Is there just one gunman?"

"Hard to tell. There could be others hiding behind the trees."

Yeah, and they had to anticipate that. But at least now they had a location, and that meant they could come up with a plan.

"The gunman's expecting me to show in fifteen minutes," Boone added. "What should I do?"

"Wait until you hear from me," Grayson ordered. He slapped the phone shut and looked at each of them. "Arm yourselves. We'll move on foot to the cemetery, but you'll stay back. I'll go in and try to negotiate their release."

The cemetery was a good mile and a half away. Still on Ryland land but outside the security fence that rimmed the ranch. And therefore not part of the surveillance system. No way to visually check what was going on. Plus, there was a problem with just driving in there—someone was no doubt watching the road.

"I got an ID on the gunman," Kade called out. "Sylvester Greer. He's a pro."

Mason hadn't expected anything less. "Any idea who hired him?"

"None," Kade answered. He hurried away from his computer and went to the weapons cabinet in the corner of the room. "But I'm betting we'll find out before the night's over."

Yeah, they would. But hopefully learning that wouldn't come at a sky-high price.

Like losing Eve.

"The gunman told you not to come," Mason reminded his brother.

Grayson spared him a glance as he, too, went to the weapons cabinet and took out magazines of ammo that he shoved into his pockets. "Would you stay back if they had Abbie?"

Mason hadn't seen that question coming, but he knew the answer was no. He wouldn't stay back. And he turned to let her know just that.

But Abbie wasn't there.

He tore out of the room and into the foyer. "Abbie?" Mason shouted.

No answer. And then he cursed when he looked at the equipment bag. The bulletproof vest was missing, and the front door was wide-open.

Chapter Eighteen

Abbie knew she didn't have much time. Probably less than a minute. She'd left the moment Mason ended the call with Boone and then had sneaked past Rusty, who was standing guard on the side of the ranch house. But it wouldn't be long before Mason or someone else realized she was missing, and they would try and stop her.

The night air was chilly, and the wind whipped at her, but she ran through the pasture. Toward the cemetery. And she tried not to think about how Mason was going to react to her leaving.

He wouldn't like it, that's for sure.

But there's no way she was going to put Grayson's wife and son at further risk, and the Rylands were too heroic to toss her in the line of fire. That heroism could endanger Eve and the baby far more than necessary.

All the danger and attacks had been leading up to this, and Abbie didn't intend to let anyone else face down a killer who was aiming for her. Well, for starters. If Ford Herrington got his death wish, then all the Ryland males would soon be in the line of fire.

Unless she could stop it.

This wasn't a suicide mission. That's why she'd put on the bulletproof vest and had brought a gun with her. She didn't have the aim of a professional hit man, but she had something that a hired gun didn't—the will to end this before Mason or any other member of his family got hurt.

That included Boone.

Yes, it was a long shot, but if Boone or she could take out the gunman, then this would finally end tonight. And she did have a little time on that front. Ford wanted her to die in front of Boone, and that meant the gunman would wait for Boone to arrive before he started firing. The gunman didn't know that Boone was already there, and unlike her, Boone had a deadly aim. If she could draw out the assassin, then maybe Boone could do the rest.

Abbie ran faster but kept glancing over her shoulder. No sign of Mason yet. She didn't have a clear view of the ranch road, but she couldn't see headlights either. Maybe the car that was supposed to whisk her away hadn't arrived yet.

When she made it to the back of the pasture, she ducked behind one of the white wooden fence posts. It wasn't wide enough to cover her, but it would have to do. She already had the gun drawn, but she got ready in case she had to take aim quickly. That would be a worst-case scenario, and it wouldn't get Eve and the baby out of danger.

She tried to pick through the darkness and the dense clump of trees so she could see the cemetery. Again, the angle was wrong. She couldn't see Eve, the baby, Boone or any gunman. She spotted one lone marble headstone. An eerie sight in the milky moonlight, especially with the wind fanning the veiny tree branches above it. Ford was one sick man to want his death wish carried out here.

Abbie levered herself up and heard the sound of footsteps. Not from the cemetery but from behind her. Before she could even look over her shoulder, someone grabbed her, hard, and shoved her to the ground.

She turned, ready for a fight, but thanks to the moonlight she had no trouble seeing her attacker's face.

Mason.

"What the hell do you think you're doing?" he snarled.

He was whispering, but Abbie could feel the anger in every muscle in his body. And there was a lot of him to feel because he literally had her pinned to the ground.

"I'm trying to save Eve and the baby," she fired back.

"This is *not* the way to do it." Mason didn't look at her. His gaze slashed all around them. With good reason. At least one gunman was out there, and he might see or hear the commotion.

"Don't move," he ordered, and he looked behind him.

Abbie did, too, and spotted several armed men making their way across the pasture. His brothers, no doubt. They were keeping low, but she could make out the silhouettes of their weapons.

She put her mouth right next to Mason's ear. "If the gunman sees all of you, he could hurt Eve. Let me go in there and try to defuse this."

"You can't defuse it. This is a death trap, and Greer, the hired gun, doesn't care a thimble of spit whether Eve and the baby get hurt in the cross fire."

Abbie wanted to argue. She definitely didn't want to think of a baby in this kind of danger. But Mason was right. Ford had set up these rules, and he wouldn't care who else died.

Oh, God.

What now?

"You're staying put," Mason insisted as if he'd heard her unspoken question. "Kade and Gage will figure out how to disarm the booby traps."

That sounded like a good start, but Abbie had to shake her head. "When the car arrives to pick me up, the driver will tell the gunman I'm not there. He'll be suspicious. And he'll know we're onto him."

"Then we have to work fast." Mason didn't hesitate, which meant he'd no doubt thought of this. "Any idea where Boone is?"

She shook her head. "I can't see Eve or the baby either."

"The picture of her and the baby was taken by my mother's grave. It's behind those." He pointed toward the thick clump of trees that were only about twenty yards from the fence.

Abbie groaned. If they were still there, it would be nearly impossible to sneak up on them. And that was no doubt the killer's intention.

"Wait here," Mason told her. "And that's an order. Move, and there'll be hell to pay."

Abbie didn't doubt that. But she wouldn't stay hidden if there was some way she could help. Of course, the trick would be to figure out how to do that without putting anyone else in even more danger.

Mason levered himself off her but then dropped right back down. Abbie followed his gaze and saw the movement to the far right of that clump of trees. It was a man. And for a moment she thought it was Boone. But it wasn't.

It was Ferguson.

Of course. So, he'd been the one to take Ford up on the offer to kill them. The money alone would have been enticing enough, but this was his chance to kill her and Boone, the man who'd protected her all these years.

Mason lifted his gun and took aim at Ferguson. He didn't fire, probably because he was waiting for the man to move a little. After all, Eve and the baby were likely just on the other side of those trees, and if Mason missed, one of them could be hit.

Abbie waited, her breath frozen in her throat. Her heart slamming against her chest.

But Ferguson didn't budge.

"What's he doing?" she mumbled. He wasn't looking toward the ranch. Nor toward the road. He seemed to focused on the cemetery itself.

That's when it hit Abbie. It was probably where Boone s hiding out.

She watched in horror as Ferguson took aim. She nted to shout out a warning. But couldn't. She could ly watch, wait and pray that Boone, Eve and the baby re out of the line of fire.

The seconds crawled by, making the wait unbearable.

Without warning, Ferguson suddenly dropped to the ound. Abbie shook her head, wondering why the heck 'd done that. But she didn't have time to wonder long.

A bullet slammed through the air.

Not toward Ferguson.

But at Mason and her.

ASON HELD HIS BREATH. Waited for another shot to come ging their way. Especially because the last one had torn o the fence. This was exactly what Mason had hoped d prayed they could avoid.

Gunfire.

He tried to crawl over Abbie to keep her down, but e maneuvered to the side and took aim. Good grief, the man was stubborn, but if their situations had been re- rsed, he sure wouldn't have stayed put either. Too bad bie was going to have to choke down her instincts and de because he didn't want her in any more danger.

"Get down!" Mason insisted.

Abbie did lower herself, slightly, and like him, she ked around to pinpoint the origin of that single shot. It d come from the general direction of where he'd spot- Ferguson. However, Abbie's nemesis was nowhere in

sight now. Probably because he'd fired that shot and th
gotten down.

Mason glanced around to make sure everyone w
okay. He could see just the outlines of his brothers wl
were scattered around the pasture. Six guns, plus Abb
Mason had wanted more, but he couldn't leave the wiv
and kids unprotected at the house. That's why he'd ask
every available ranch hand to stand guard outside the ran
house.

"Listen," Abbie whispered, her voice trembling now

And Mason knew why. He heard the same sounds s
had. The baby. Crying. Grayson no doubt heard it, too, a
there was no way he would continue to lie in wait in t
pasture with his son's cries filling the night air. No. Th
could get even more dangerous, fast.

Abbie apparently thought so, too, because she shout
out before Mason could stop her. "You said you'd let E
and the baby go if I came. Well, here I am. Now let the
go."

Mason braced himself for a shot to come their wa
But it didn't.

"Come out where I can see you," the person shout
back. Mason recognized the man's voice from the earli
phone call. It was almost certainly Greer.

"You're not going to do this," Mason told her, and
latched on to her arm just in case she tried. He should ha
clamped a hand over her mouth.

"I'll come out there when Eve and the baby are safe
away from all this," Abbie answered.

Silence. But Mason kept watch while he waited f
Greer to respond.

Where the devil was Ferguson? Was he trying to sne
up on them? Maybe. But it could be worse than that. Mas
had no idea how many other gunmen were working wi

Greer and Ferguson, and here Abbie was willing to walk right into the middle of that viper's nest.

"I'm coming out," someone else shouted. Not Greer this time but Boone. "You can release Eve and baby and hold me at gunpoint instead. Abbie will do whatever you tell her if you're holding me. Isn't that right, Abbie?"

"Stay back, Boone!" she yelled. And she no doubt meant it. She was terrified for his life.

But Mason saw this from a different point of the view. From Ferguson's. If he had Boone, he did indeed control Abbie, and it'd be easier to kill them both.

"All right," Greer answered. "Boone, you have a deal. Come out so I can see you, and keep your hands in the air."

"No!" Abbie shouted. But it was too late.

Mason saw Boone step from the clump of trees. Not too far from where he'd spotted Ferguson earlier. Mason couldn't see Greer, but he had no doubt that the assassin had his weapon trained on Boone.

"They're coming out," Greer announced.

"What about the booby traps?" Grayson yelled.

Greer took his time answering. "Eve knows where she has to run."

Oh, mercy. It was dark, and Eve was scared. Not the best of conditions for navigating what could be a minefield.

Mason held his breath. Waited. Prayed. Hoped that if his prayer failed, his aim wouldn't.

Boone moved to his right and eventually out of sight. On Greer's orders probably. Finally, Mason saw something he actually wanted to see.

Eve and the baby.

His sister-in-law had a crying Chet clutched to her chest, and she ran out from the trees. Grayson got up and raced over the fence toward them.

Mason and his brothers responded, too. They all approached, ready to fire if anyone took a shot at Grayson. Thank God that didn't happen. Grayson helped them over the fence and pulled them down to the ground so he could shield them. The next step would be to get them completely away from there.

Abbie, too.

But that thought had no sooner crossed his mind, when there was movement in the trees again. Mason could see Boone, and he appeared to be arguing, but he couldn't make out what he was saying.

"Eve and the baby should go now," Greer ordered.

Grayson lifted his head, looked around. No doubt wondering if it was a trap.

"Just the two of them," Greer clarified. "Not her husband. Not Abbie. Not anyone else. And hey, if I'd wanted them dead, they wouldn't be out there with you."

True, but Mason didn't trust Greer or the snake who'd hired him.

"Go now, Eve!" Greer insisted. "Last chance to get that baby away from here before all hell breaks loose."

Grayson gave her a nod, and she started moving. She stayed low. Kept the baby close to her. She made her way back to the house.

"Oh, God," Abbie mumbled.

Just as Boone dived to the side.

There was no time to figure out why he did that because the shots started, and one of them slammed into the fence right next to Abbie and Mason. As close as that shot was, Mason still took a moment to glance back, to make sure Eve and the baby were out of harm's way.

They were.

That was something, at least. Now he had to do the same for Abbie by taking out the shooter.

Shooters, Mason corrected.

There were two sets of shots, and both were coming right at them. Greer and Ferguson probably. But where was Boone, and was he in a position to help?

"What happened to your plan of taking me?" Abbie shouted over the shots.

"Stay quiet," Mason warned her so the shooters couldn't pinpoint their position, but he wanted to know the same darn thing.

"This is the plan," Greer calmly answered.

None of them responded. They just waited. But Mason suddenly got a very bad feeling in the pit of his stomach.

"You'll stand up, climb over the fence and come stand by your grandfather's grave. That's where Ford requested that you all die."

Yeah, Ford was a sick SOB all right. "Any reason we'd just walk to our slaughter?" Mason asked, figured the answer he was about to hear was obvious.

Ferguson and Greer were going to use Boone to lure them out.

Not the wisest of plans, especially because all but Abbie hated him. Well, maybe not hate. But there was no love lost there. Maybe their attackers were counting on the fact that six lawmen weren't just going to stand by while Boone was gunned down.

"You've got no leverage," Boone called out to the gunmen. "I won't have any of my sons or Abbie dying because of me."

"Oh, it's not you they'll try to save." And Greer let that hang in the air for several bad moments.

"What do you mean?" Grayson finally asked.

"I mean your wife is wearing a jacket with an explosive device. She's probably inside the house now with all the others. The wives, the kids, the ranch hands. And even if he's taken off the jacket, the device is still there."

Oh, hell. And Mason just kept repeating it. Across from him, he heard Grayson utter something much worse.

"All of you, stand up now," Greer ordered. "Drop your weapons, put your hands in the air so I can see them. And start walking toward me. One wrong move, and I detonate the explosive, and everybody in that house dies.

"Oh," Greer said, his tone mocking, "you've got thirty seconds."

Chapter Nineteen

"Stay behind me," Mason warned Abbie.

She would for now, but they both knew that wouldn't last long. Soon, Greer would want her since she was first on the list.

"Put down your guns," Greer reminded them.

Abbie dropped hers, lifted her hands into the air. Mason dropped his, too, but Abbie saw the pistol he had tucked in the back waist of his jeans. He didn't remove that one, but he did lift his hands and started over the fence.

"Behind me," Mason emphasized to her.

Abbie did that, as well. She climbed over the fence, along with the others, and they started trudging toward the cemetery.

"Those thirty seconds are almost up," Greer taunted.

That got them hurrying, even though Abbie hated that Greer was playing with them like puppets. Still, they couldn't risk an explosion. They all came to a stop in the clearing, just a few feet away from the first grave.

Boone was already there, waiting for them to join him.

It took a moment for her to spot Greer because he was partly hidden behind a tree. And armed, of course.

"You sent a text to your wife," Greer accused, looking directly at Grayson. "Don't bother to deny it," he continued when Grayson didn't answer. "It's all right if you told her about the device. I'm getting paid to finish things with all of you, not them."

Despite the circumstances, Abbie believed him, and she was glad that Grayson had managed to warn Eve. Maybe now the Ryland wives and children would be safe. That was something, at least.

Greer pointed to one of the trees on Abbie's left, and when she followed his pointing finger, she spotted the rifleman perched on one of the branches. That explained the two sets of shots.

Well, maybe.

"Where's Ferguson?" Abbie just came right out and asked. "Or does he plan to stay in hiding when he shoots me?"

"He's not going to shoot you," Boone growled. And like Mason, he also stepped in front of her.

However, the shift in position didn't block her from seeing Greer's reaction. He certainly wasn't jumping to answer, and he seemed annoyed. She hoped that meant Greer and Ferguson weren't seeing eye to eye on how this should all play out. Dissention could work in her favor.

Greer pointed to two other trees. "Cameras," he explained. "Senator Herrington left the money for this job in the hands of an attorney in the Cayman Islands, and the lawyer requires proof."

Mason glared at the cameras, at the gunman in the tree and at Greer. "I hope your boss is paying you enough to have this much blood on your hands."

"Who says I have a boss, other than the late senator, that is?" Greer fired back.

Mason shrugged. "You're not smart enough to set this up on your own."

Abbie gave Mason a warning groan, which he ignored

Maybe he figured he could goad Greer into doing something that would violate the rules of this nightmare.

"Besides, Ford left only three letters," Mason continued, "and you didn't get one of them." He put his hands on his hips, close to his gun. "But it does make me wonder—will your boss keep you alive? Because I gotta say, you are a major loose end that could tie you to multiple murders and a boatload of other felonies."

"Yeah," Gage chimed in. "And because your boss isn't showing his face, then I'm thinking he wants you to do all the dirty work. Then he takes out you and your wingman in the tree, sends the video to the lawyer, and he doesn't have to pay you a penny."

Even in the darkness, Abbie saw the anger flash over Greer's face. "That's not going to happen." He turned that anger on Mason. "And time's up. Step to the side."

So that Greer could kill her.

Mason would try and stop that from happening. So would Boone. Abbie, too. But she doubted all of them would make it out of this alive, and she darn sure didn't want someone else dying in her place.

Abbie glanced at Mason, making eye contact, even though she could see him inching his hand toward his gun. He didn't have to tell her what he wanted her to do. He wanted her to get down while he had a shootout with Greer and the rifleman.

In other words, suicide.

Abbie snapped toward Greer. She figured she had seconds, or less, to try to stop that from happening. "I don't want to die in front of the Rylands," she told Greer. Not a lie but the next part was. "I have no connection with any of them other than through Boone, and they haven't exactly given me a warm and fuzzy welcome to Silver Creek."

Mason shot her a glare, which she ignored.

"Ford's instructions were that I was to die in front of Boone," she continued. "*Just* Boone."

That wasn't an amused look Greer gave her. More like a suspicious one. He paused for several seconds. Then, he shook his head. "No deal. All of you stay together. And you die together. One at a time."

Abbie had expected that response, but she wasn't giving up.

Greer aimed his gun directly at her. She got ready to dive to the side. Away from Mason and Boone. And she hoped they did the same.

Everything happened fast but in slow motion, too. She saw Greer's hand tense, ready to pull the trigger. But before he could do that, Mason rammed his body into hers, sending her crashing to the ground.

A shot cracked through the air.

But Abbie couldn't tell who had shot or where the bullet had landed. That's because Mason dropped right on top of her, and the fall and the impact knocked the breath out of her.

There was another shot. Then another. But Abbie couldn't move because she was gasping for air. Mason, however, moved her. He dragged her behind one of the trees, and he came up to return fire.

Abbie heard the sound then. Not just a bullet. But the deadly thud of a bullet slamming into something. Into *someone,* she mentally corrected. There was a groan of pain.

And then nothing.

With her heart racing out of control, she looked at Mason. He had ducked behind the tree but was also still firing. He wasn't hurt, thank God. Well, not yet anyway.

She frantically looked around for Boone. No sign of

him. And she hated to have to consider that he might have been the one who was shot. If not him, then one of his sons.

"I have to take out the rifleman," Mason mumbled. "Don't move," he ordered her again.

Abbie couldn't anyway. She was still fighting for breath. Plus, going out there now would only get Mason and her killed.

Mason scrambled to the next tree over, then another, and Abbie got her first glimpse of the war zone playing out in front of her. Grayson was behind one of the trees, and he, too, had taken aim at the rifleman. She was thankful that Grayson had a gun as well, but that wasn't stopping the rifleman. He was firing nonstop, and he definitely had a better vantage point.

She shifted a little, still keeping cover behind the tree but also searching for Boone. No sign of him or Mason's other brothers. Definitely no sign of the person who'd been shot. It was too much to hope that it'd been Greer or Ferguson.

Abbie thought of the Ryland wives back at the house and prayed that none of them would try to come into this. Of course, that was a strong possibility. She imagined herself in their place, with the men they loved in danger, and Abbie knew there was no way she could stay put.

With her breath level again, she searched around the tree for something, anything, she could use as a weapon. She latched on to a small limb and was dragging it closer when she saw the movement from the corner of her eye.

There was no time for her to react. No time to get out of the way. Something bashed right into her head. The pain was instant. Searing. And before Abbie could even call out to Mason, the darkness came.

MASON CURSED. THE RIFLEMAN was out of range of Mason's Colt. Probably the reason the would-be killer had chosen that particular spot in the first place. Not good. Because as long as he stayed in that tree, none of them were safe.

He glanced around, trying to work out everyone's position, but the only one he could see was Grayson. When the shots had started, everyone had scattered, and Mason only hoped that one of them was in a better position than he was to eliminate the rifleman.

"Abbie?" he heard someone shout. Boone.

Mason swung his gaze in her direction. And his heart went to his knees. He saw her all right, but she was being dragged into the bushes. Oh, mercy. Had she been shot? Or worse?

But Mason refused to believe that.

"Abbie!" he shouted. Mason ignored the rifleman and ran toward the spot where she'd disappeared into the thick underbrush.

She didn't answer, and that revved up his heartbeat even more. He wanted to call out her name again, but that wasn't a wise choice. Her captor could use the sound of Mason's voice to aim and take Mason out. That couldn't happen. If Mason got shot, he couldn't save, and it was clear that Abbie needed saving.

Staying low, Mason shoved some of the underbrush aside. No Abbie. It was too dark to follow the drag marks, and the gunfight was drowning out sounds that he needed to hear.

What the devil was going on? Had Greer managed to take her? If so, it wasn't hard to figure out why. According to Ford's rule, Abbie had to die in front of Boone. Greer wouldn't just give up on the kind of money he was earning for this. No. He and maybe even his boss were still trying to set up the kill.

And Mason had to stop it.

He tore his way through the underbrush and came to

some trees that rimmed the west part of the cemetery. Where his mother's grave was located.

Where Greer would try to kill Abbie.

But there were no signs of either of them here.

However, Mason did hear something. He tried to pick through the din of gunfire to pinpoint the low sound he'd heard. A moan. But not just an ordinary moan.

This was one of pain.

He tried not to panic. Hard to do when it could be Abbie who'd made that sound. Abbie, in pain. Mason scrambled to the side and nearly tripped over something.

Except it wasn't a something.

It was a *someone*.

The moonlight helped him, and Mason looked down at the twisted face of Vernon Ferguson. The front of the man's shirt looked shiny black, but Mason knew it was blood.

He'd been shot.

Ferguson clutched Mason's arm. "I didn't do this," he got out.

Mason made a yeah-right sound, and he picked up the gun by Ferguson's side, but something wasn't right. After all, Ferguson had been shot. He was dying.

And someone had done this to him.

"If you didn't put this plan together, then why are you here?" Mason demanded.

"Greer called and said if I wanted to watch Abbie die, I should come."

"Hard to believe that's the only reason. Did Greer decide to kill you—his boss—and collect the money for himself?" Mason asked. He didn't look at Ferguson. He kept watch around him in case this was some kind of ambush.

"I'm not his boss." Ferguson's mouth stretched into a creepy smile. "I wanted to keep Abbie alive. It's more fun when she's alive."

Mason shook his head. In some sick twisted way, that made sense. Ferguson couldn't torment a dead woman. Did that mean Greer was working alone? Maybe. But it didn't matter. Greer and the rifleman were just as dangerous.

He had to get to Abbie.

"Where is she?" Mason demanded, and he threw off Ferguson's grip.

Ferguson shook his head, and Mason knew he couldn't waste any more time. With his gun in one hand and Ferguson's in the other, Mason ran toward the clearing. Toward his mother's grave.

And that's when he saw Abbie.

She was alive, thank God, but there was blood trickling down the side of her face. In the pale moonlight, she looked like a ghost.

Mason started to run to her. But he came to a dead stop. Because Abbie wasn't alone. Someone was standing behind her.

And that someone had a gun pointed directly at her head.

EVERYTHING WAS SWIMMING in and out of focus, but Abbie blinked, trying to fight her way out of the arm that was vised around her neck. Hard to do with the blow to the head. It had not only made her temporarily lose consciousness, she was now woozy and weak.

Who was behind her? Who had the gun to her head?

Greer probably. And she was betting he didn't intend to keep her alive much longer.

"Let her go," she heard Mason say. His voice was low, a dangerous growl, and despite the gunfire on the other side of the cemetery, she had no trouble hearing him.

Or seeing him.

Every muscle in his face and body was rock hard.

Primed for a fight. But it didn't take a clear head for her to know that he didn't have a shot. Not with her captor using her as a human shield.

"Stay put, Mason," her captor called out. "Boone, get out here now!"

For a moment Abbie thought her injury had caused her mind to play tricks on her ears. She'd expected Greer's voice, but it wasn't.

It was Rodney Stone's.

"You don't have to do this," Mason said. "There are other ways to get money."

"Not Ford's money," Stone fired back. "He was my friend, and he would expect me to do this for him."

Abbie groaned. So it wasn't just about the money. It might have been easier to talk him out of it if it had been.

"Boone?" Stone shouted again. "The camera's waiting for you."

Abbie glanced up and saw the camera mounted in the tree. It was pointed directly at her.

"Get out here now or I shoot Mason," Stone warned.

"You're planning to shoot me anyway," Mason countered, and he inched forward, his gun aimed and ready in case he got a clear shot.

"True," Stone verified. "But I can make it quick and painless. Or I can make you suffer. Make Abbie suffer, too."

The threat went through her. And Mason. She could see the fear on his face. The raw frustration, as well. He couldn't stop this, and it was killing him.

Abbie wasn't ready to say goodbye to Mason just yet, but she had to accept that it was exactly what she might have to do. And it broke her heart. It had taken her more than three decades to fall in love, and here she'd had only minutes to savor it.

"Boone!" Stone yelled again. He moved the gun to Abbie's belly. "How long will it take her to bleed out? Get out here now or you'll learn the answer to that the hard way."

Mason took a step closer. "You set the fire at the ranch?" he asked.

The question threw her, and judging from the way Stone's arm tense, it threw him, too. "Why the hell would that matter now?"

"Because I want to know why I'm about to die." Mason kept his eyes trained on Stone. "I figure the fire was to draw Boone out. It was the fastest way to get him to Silver Creek."

"You want a gold star, Deputy?" Stone mocked. "Because I'm fresh out of them. And Boone's fresh out of time."

Stone was ready to pull the trigger. Abbie had no doubt about that, and while the shot probably wouldn't kill her, she braced herself for the pain that she would feel. And the pain she would see on Mason's face.

There was movement to her right. It happened so fast that Abbie only got a glimpse of Boone before he dived right at them. He crashed into them, sending all three of them to the ground.

Stone fired, the sound of the bullet so close that it was deafening.

Abbie rolled to the side, trying to move away from Stone's gun. She also tried to move Mason and Boone out of the way.

She failed.

Mason was there, right in the tangle of bodies. Fists were flying. Blood splattered across her face, but she had no idea whose it was.

Abbie reached out and held Stone's hand so he couldn't fire again.

But it was too late.

He fired.

The blast went through her, and it took her a moment to realize she hadn't been hit.

Boone had.

Stone's shot went straight into Boone's chest.

Abbie heard herself scream, and she tried to get to him. She failed at that, too. Stone lifted the gun again, ready to kill Mason.

But the other shot came first.

The moment seemed to freeze. She glanced at Mason. Then at the gun in Boone's hand. The one he'd just used to shoot Stone.

Stone fell back, his eyes wide-open and lifeless.

Because the world was starting to spin around, Abbie would have fallen, too, but Mason was right there to catch her in his arms.

Chapter Twenty

Mason handed Abbie the small carton of orange juice that he'd gotten from the vending machine. "You should drink something," he insisted.

She looked up at him from the seat in the surgical waiting room. Her eyes were glazed with fatigue. Her shoulders, slumped. It had been a long night, and the end wasn't in sight yet because Boone was in surgery, and the initial report was that he was in critical condition from Stone's gunshot wound.

A wound that could ultimately kill him.

"You should drink something, too," she insisted right back.

Mason held up his cup of black coffee for her to see. It was his third.

She managed a frown. "Something healthier."

He would do that. Later. Maybe they could have a big family breakfast, especially because all his brothers, their wives, the kids, their nannies and even Bessie were scattered around the room. All waiting for Boone to get out of surgery.

His father, Mason mentally corrected.

Because he had certainly come through for them tonight. He'd saved Abbie, and Mason would be eternally grateful to him for that. It didn't erase the past. Or the hurt. But it was a start.

"Mel just finished questioning Nicole," Dade told everyone after finishing yet another call. His brother had taken over tying up the loose ends of the investigation. Good thing, too, because Mason just wasn't up to it.

It would take a while for him to get over how close Abbie had come to dying tonight. Grayson clearly felt the same about Eve and his baby because he had both of them in his lap and was holding on for dear life. Gage was doing pretty much the same to Lynette.

"It doesn't look as if Nicole had anything to do with this," Dade added. "Nor Ferguson."

Mason agreed. Ferguson was dead but had used his dying breath to say he hadn't been involved. Even though Ferguson was a slimy snake, there had been no reason for him to lie at that point. Plus, even if he had, it didn't matter. He'd died on the way to the hospital. The man was no longer a threat to Abbie or anyone else.

Abbie opened the orange juice, took a sip and handed it to him. Mason surrendered and put his coffee on the floor so he could drink. It tasted like acid, probably because his stomach was still churning.

She took his hand and drew him down into the seat next to her. Mason went one step further and slipped her arm around him so he could pull her closer. His brothers would notice.

But he didn't care.

He brushed a kiss on her forehead. Then her cheek. And what the heck. He kissed her. In hindsight, he wished he'd done it sooner because the heat from the kiss melted some of that ice in his blood.

When he finally pulled back, Abbie made a small sound

of approval and eased right back into his arms. "Don't sell the paint mare."

Now, that was not something Mason expected to hear her say. He cocked his head so he could meet her gaze. And her second frown of the past five minutes.

"It settles my mind to think of the horses and the ranch," she mumbled as if he would understand.

And he did. Because it was exactly how he felt. The ranch was what centered him. Always had. Well, until now. It disturbed him a little to think that the kiss with Abbie had done the same thing. Maybe better.

"The only person who can handle the mare is you," Mason pointed out. He hadn't intended that to sound like an invitation with strings attached.

But it was.

She stared at him. "Does that mean I have my job back?"

He stared back at her. "As a minimum."

A really low minimum.

Mason realized he had things to say to her, but he needed to lay some groundwork first. "We'll need to get official approval from Marshal McKinney, but with Ferguson and Stone out of the picture, there's no reason for you to go back into witness protection."

"So I could work with the mare." Abbie nodded. Paused. Her mouth quivered a little. "Would I get to sleep with the boss?"

Okay. The groundwork was going pretty darn fast. "As often as you want."

Now she smiled. "Good, because I'd like that *often*." She slipped her hand around the back of his neck, drew him closer and kissed him.

She tasted like sunshine, and Mason didn't think the juice was responsible for that.

"Who's the gunman?" he asked.

She shook her head. "I don't know."

"And you thought it was okay to bring this kind of danger to the ranch without warning anyone? Someone other than you could have been killed tonight."

He knew that sounded gruff, insensitive even. But no one had ever accused him of putting sensitivity first. Still, he felt…something. Something he cursed, too. Because Mason hated the fear in Abbie's voice. Hated even more the vulnerability he saw in her eyes.

Oh, man.

This was a damsel-in-distress reaction. He could face down a cold-blooded killer and not flinch. But a woman in pain was something he had a hard time stomaching. Especially this woman.

He blamed that on her flimsy gown. And cursed again.